Cover Design: Steamy Designs

Cover Photo: lindee robinson

Cover models: Fatima Kojima & Jordan Guske

edited by: Tasha L. Harrison

Every story is for my mom, who made me fall in love with reading & Ms. K, who made me fall in love with writing.

Memories
are precious!
happy reading.

♡
Lucy
Eden
2020

CHERISHING THE GODDESS

Billionaire CEO Alexander Wolfe has spent years putting in 120-hour weeks and adding zeroes to his net worth. But lately, work has left him feeling burnt out and uninspired. Then he is given the chance to go head-to-head with a legendary corporate raider and the man he'd idolized his entire career. He seizes the opportunity, immediately jumping on a plane for Barbados to close the deal in person. If he's successful, it'll be the biggest win of his career.

He had no way of knowing that meeting a mesmerizing beauty would have the power to derail everything...

Calypso Sterling has no time for men who value her beauty over her intellect. Instead, she focuses all her energy on her studies and career aspirations. But when her home—and a closely guarded family secret—is threatened, she's ready to defend all she holds dear.

She had no way of knowing a handsome stranger had the power to take away everything she'd ever loved...

This standalone, workplace/ enemies to lovers romance features characters from Everything's Better With Kimberly, is full of alphas and steam and has NO cheating.

This is the novelized, extended version of the previously published novella of the same name.

CHERISHING THE GODDESS

LUCY EDEN

❧

ONE

"*H*ey, John!"

"What do you want, you little creep?" A smile tugged at my lips. I was sitting on the balcony of my one bedroom luxury suite in front of my open laptop. I've been at the Sterling three weeks. It was initially a work trip, but the longer I spent on the island, the more it felt like something else.

The voice belonged to Philip, the eight-year-old interloper who I'd met during one of my many walks around the resort. I checked into The Sterling under an assumed name three weeks ago, and my new little friend had spent almost every day of the last week making a habit of rudely interrupting my daily morning routine of gym and coffee followed by hours of reading legal briefs and interpreting reports.

"I want to kick your sorry arse again," he shouted up to

me while holding a soccer ball over his head, John Cusack in *Say Anything* style.

"You kiss your mother with that mouth?" I barked a laugh at the kid's sass and leaned away from my computer.

Philip looked around carefully, no doubt checking to be sure his mother wasn't around, and I knew that I was going to appreciate his next words. A sly grin spread across his face.

"No, but I kissed *your* mother with this mouth." He waggled his eyebrows.

I shook my head and laughed again.

"Get out of here, kid. I have a lot of work to do today." I did have a lot of work, too much work.

"But it's Saturday. You're not supposed to work on the weekends." He was still too young to understand that the world didn't stop spinning because of a day on the calendar. That's a lesson I knew all too well at his age. There was always work to be done, and there was always someone waiting to take your job.

"I work every day. Where's your old man? Ask him to play with you."

Philip's face fell, and he dropped the soccer ball at his side.

"He's working too. He told my mum and me that he was taking us on holiday to spend time with us, but he's always on his mobile." He looked down at his feet and kicked the ground.

Well, that did it. I started closing the files on my computer.

Philip's career aspirations were a mystery to me, but he had a very bright future as a con man because he knew the right buttons to push. I lost my parents when I was a little younger than he was and was raised by my father's parents. I inherited my grandfather's work ethic, but it wasn't something I appreciated when I was Philip's age.

"All right, you little weasel. I'll be right down." I shut my laptop just in time to see an excited grin spread on Philip's face. It didn't help that the kid reminded me of myself at that age: skinny, dark hair and blue eyes. He was well cared for with the faintest air of neglect that kids who were raised wealthy with absentee parents recognized in each other.

I ran down the stairs, snatched the ball out of Philip's hand, and took off running to the field next to a cluster of buildings that housed the luxury suites.

"Hey!" he squealed and ran after me.

I dropped the ball at my feet and passed it to Philip. He kicked it back.

"Do your parents know where you are?"

"No. They don't care."

"I don't know about that." I pulled my phone from the pocket of my shorts. "Why don't you let them know, so they don't worry." I dialed the concierge.

"All right," he muttered and gave me his parent's names. I

recognized his dad's name as a corporate attorney based in London who my company had dealings with a few years ago, making his mother the former model that he left his first wife for. I was connected and handed the phone off when it rang.

"Hi, Mummy," he said. "Yes, I'm all right. I'm playing football with a friend." He looked up at me. "I'm at the pitch." He heaved a deep sigh. "Okay. I love you too, Mummy."

I smirked at his *perfect little prince* act. Where was the foul-mouthed little runt who interrupted me on my balcony?

The field we were on couldn't really be called a soccer pitch. It was too small, and there were other guests having picnics, sunbathing and flying kites.

So this is what people do on Saturdays, I thought to myself.

I found myself staring at a man about my age as he tossed a toddler in the air. A woman, who might have been his wife, watched them while smoothing a hand over a round, pregnant belly. I felt a tug on my shirt.

"Thank you." Philip handed me my phone.

"Everything okay, little man?"

He nodded and kicked the grass. "She's coming to get me when she's done getting her massage."

"Okay, well until then," I said trying to lighten the mood. "Whatcha got, superstar?"

His face brightened, his eyes narrowed, and he kicked the ball to me.

We passed that ball back and forth for a few minutes when I noticed we had an audience.

A beautiful woman with long dark curly hair was standing about twenty feet away watching our soccer match with interest. She was engaged in conversation with an older woman, but she kept glancing over at us. Whenever her eyes met mine she looked away. I felt my heart tug.

"Hey, John." Philip's words registered in my brain a split second before the ball hit me in the stomach catching me off guard and eliciting a loud grunt. Philip burst out laughing. I glanced at our observer who was no longer looking at us but was suppressing a smile. She'd seen everything.

"You should kiss *her*," he teased.

"That's not how it works, kid. You don't just go around kissing people you don't know." I passed the ball to him. "And you're going to be sorry for that." I laughed before he stuck his tongue out at me.

We resumed our game, and I tried to refrain from sneaking glances at her, with little success. Philip noticed, shot me one of his mischievous grins and before I could stop him, he kicked the ball in her direction as hard as he could.

"You little…" I narrowed my eyes at him before turning to jog to her to retrieve the ball. Before I could reach her, she pointed her toe at the oncoming sphere, let it roll up her shin and into the air. She dribbled it from one knee to the other a few times before letting it hit the ground where she kicked it back to Philip with precision. The kid and I froze with our mouths hanging open. She shot Philip a grin and winked at him before resuming her conversation. I never thought I'd find myself jealous of an eight-year-old but there I was wishing she'd aimed that smile at me.

"Pip, darling. There you are." I turned around to see a woman with long sleek brown hair, wearing giant sunglasses, wrapping her arms around Philip.

"Pip?" I mouthed at him giving him a skeptical look. He narrowed his eyes at me and, out of his mother's line of sight, flashed me what would be a peace symbol in New York, but I knew meant something very different in London. I huffed out a silent chuckle.

I glanced at our admirer who again had caught the entire exchange and was wearing an amused look.

Pip's mother straightened up and turned to face me. Her eyes roamed my body before she removed her sunglasses, stood straighter, pushed her shoulders back and tossed her hair over her shoulder, making me wonder if Philip was the only person his dad was neglecting on this vacation.

"Pip, darling." Her voice was higher, and every sentence was punctuated with a giggle. "Is this the friend you were playing football with?"

"Yes, Mummy," he replied in a bored tone. "This is John."

"Well, John. Thank you so much for looking after my little Pip for me. We fly back to London tomorrow, but you must allow me to take you to dinner tonight to show my appreciation." Philip's mother lowered her chin and gazed up at me through her lashes. The offer would have been tempting if the kid wasn't standing six feet away, and if I could stop thinking about the woman standing twenty feet away. I chanced a glance at her. Our eyes met for a brief second, and she turned away, her lips forming a tight line. I took a step back. It was suddenly very important to me that she didn't get the wrong idea about this situation.

"Will your husband and son be joining us?" I had no intention of having dinner with her, but I wanted her to understand that I knew exactly how she intended to show her appreciation and that I wasn't interested.

"No." Her expression darkened for a moment but she recovered quickly and took a step forward, placing one of her hands on my bicep. "My husband will be working, and Philip has an early bedtime because he doesn't do well on planes." She ignored her son's groan of embarrassment. "So I'll be dining *alone*."

She tilted her chin up and looked into my eyes. All of her coyness was gone and pretenses dropped. I pushed her hand away.

"Well, I have other plans but no need to thank me. *Pip*," I shot Philip a glance, and he narrowed his eyes again, "is a great kid."

She pasted on a smile, bristling at my rejection.

"Come along, Pip." She patted Philip on the shoulder. "We're meeting Daddy for lunch, and we don't want to be late."

Philip grabbed his ball and followed his mother across the field before calling over his shoulder.

"Bye, John."

I waved at Philip and looked over to find the mystery woman, but she was gone.

TWO

ALEXANDER

I spent the rest of the afternoon exploring the grounds of The Sterling. I've been studying the plans, and looking at photos of the property for weeks but it didn't compare to standing under a row of fifty foot tall palm trees, smelling the salty sea air mixed with the scent of tropical flowers and hearing the ocean crash against the cliffs.

My mind kept drifting to the woman on the field. Every turn I took on a path around the property found hope swelling in my chest that I'd see her again, but I was disappointed every time.

I went back to my suite and finished working. It took a while to regain focus. My attention was being pulled to the view of the ocean outside my balcony and the memory of her smile.

That one gorgeous smile.

After a few hours, I was able to finish the reports, draft a couple of emails and had just finished the daily rundown with my executive assistant, Maggie, when Matt knocked on my door. His flight landed an hour ago so he must come here straight from the airport.

"Hey Dick," he shouted his usual greeting. "What is with this Paul Bunyan look you've got going on? You do know you're not an actual spy."

I huffed out a chuckle and scratched the three weeks of facial scruff I'd been growing.

"I don't know. I kinda like it." I walked to the fridge and pulled out two beers.

He took the beers and looked around my suite. "Jesus Christ, they didn't have any *small* luxury suites," he joked. "Your bathroom in New York is bigger than this."

"Hey, Asshole," I replied, tapping him in the gut with my fist. "The point is discretion, and I kinda like the small space. I might downsize when I get back to the city."

"Jesus fucking Christ. First the beard, then the tiny apartment. If you start talking about moving to Brooklyn and wearing suspenders, I'm having you committed."

For the first time in weeks, the thought of going back to New York made me sad. When I set foot on this island, I had a mission that didn't involve playing soccer with kids, watching the sun rise and set over the Atlantic every day and daydreaming about beautiful women who can bend it like Beckham. I was here to prepare for one of the most important meetings of my career. It wouldn't be a financial victory, but more a personal triumph. I was going head to head with Barnabas Sterling.

He was a corporate legend and a fucking shark. His nickname was "The Closer" because he could charm any reluctant seller, strong arm anyone that got in his way, and if the front door was locked, he would find a back door or kick in a window.

A little over twenty-five years ago he sold his stake in his firm and all of his international holdings and disappeared with no explanation. I was always suspicious that there was more to the story. He was in his late thirties and at the top of his game. Who would give that up and why?

A couple of years ago the real estate branch of my corporation began to invest heavily in the Caribbean. Tropical tourism is always a money maker if you choose the right island and Barbados was one of the best: a healthy economy, stable climate and because it was set so far east in The Atlantic, it hardly got any weather worse than a tropical storm.

I hardly paid attention to the Caribbean deals. My real estate team was led by Matt Widnicki, my oldest friend and a fellow Harvard grad with a brilliant mind for business. I held a bi-weekly meeting with every department head, so I can be briefed on every deal. The meetings are superfluous, but I was a control freak, and that's wasn't going to change anytime soon.

About three months ago, in one of those meetings, Matt mentioned "*a stubborn son of a bitch*" in Barbados, refusing deals for his property that anyone in their right mind would take. I didn't think anything of it and Matt didn't seem worried, just annoyed. Last month, he mentioned it again, with the name of the property, The Sterling Beachfront Paradise. It seemed like too much of a coincidence.

I did a little digging, and sure enough, The Sterling Beachfront Paradise was owned by an Amelia Sterling and her husband, Barnabas. It was the gold star standard in hospitality in Barbados with a prime location. It was built on top of a cliff on the east coast of the island. I could see why Matt wanted it so badly. We had already acquired other resorts on the island, but this was going to be the crown jewel of our Caribbean properties. And for me, the cherry on top of the sundae was the chance to close The Closer. The opportunity to go toe to toe with a legend was too good to pass up.

I could only find one photo of the guy. It was an old corporate headshot from the mid-nineties. He was young, about my age, in his early to mid-thirties. His skin was pale—no spray tans for The Closer— and his blonde hair was slicked back. He had a hard chiseled face with a square jaw. His steel gray eyes seemed to be sizing me up from my tablet screen. There were no photos of his wife either. I didn't find that unusual. I paid millions of dollars a year to keep my name out of the papers and my photos off of the internet. It was probably a lot easier and cheaper to stay under the radar back then.

My first order of business was to learn all I could about the property by checking it out myself. It's what The Closer would do. I had Maggie schedule a meeting with Sterling and flew to Barbados.

The Sterling was everything it claimed to be. My suite, which faced the ocean, was impeccably styled and spotless. The property and grounds were immaculately kept, and the staff were the friendliest and most attentive I'd ever encountered. I was supposed to be spending the last three weeks looking for flaws I could exploit and use in my negotiation, but I'd spent the last three weeks learning that I liked Barbados and missing New York and the office less and less.

"Hey, did you give any more thought to that Forbes profile?" Matt opened a beer and handed it to me.

"Nope. Not doing it," I said and took a sip. Matt didn't share my stance on privacy. My grandfather always said to let a man's work tell you who he is. He never gave interviews, never did public appearances. The only time his picture ever appeared on the company's website was when he died seven years ago. While I agreed with nearly all of my grandfather's opinions, except his political ones, the truth is, the public eye never appealed to me.

"We could crack the top fifty if you shook things up a bit."

I rolled my eyes. When I took over Wolfe Industries, we were at eighty-seven on Fortune. Now we were at sixty two. But apparently, we weren't climbing fast enough for my best friend.

"No."

"You need to get with the times, Alex. Everything is visible. Reclusive billionaires are weird. People don't trust them. You're not Batman."

"How do you know?" I growled in a Christian Bale from *The Dark Knight* impression making Matt do a spit take.

"Fucking asshole," he laughed wiping the beer off his chin with the back of his hand.

"My parents *are* dead," I reminded him. He laughed again this time almost choking on his beer.

"That was dark, man," he said through a coughing fit. "But I'm serious. Get an Instagram account. Do a TEDtalk. Date a supermodel…publicly."

I shook my head. Matt had sunk his teeth in this celebrity CEO bullshit, and experience taught me that once Matt locked his jaws on anything the only way to get him to let go was to distract him.

"Hey, you remember the lawyer from the Tolbert merger?"

"That British asshole? Yeah, why?"

I proceeded to tell him about Philip and meeting his mother on the field earlier. I left out the part about the mystery woman, but I wasn't sure why.

"Wasn't she a Victoria's Secret model? Like runway and catalog?"

"I think so." I shrugged.

"So what the fuck are you doing here?"

"Matt, her kid was with her," I scoffed. *And she wasn't the woman I really wanted.*

"Have you gotten laid once since you've been down here?"

"I've been working the whole time. So, no, I haven't."

"And the chicks will probably think you're going to beg them for change."

I chuckled and took another sip of my beer.

"You are showering regularly, right?"

"Define regularly…" I narrowed my eyes with a half-smile.

"Come on, Hobo Joe." He laughed. "I'm starving. Let's go grab some dinner."

THREE

CALYPSO

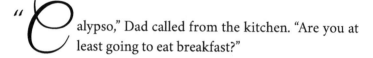alypso," Dad called from the kitchen. "Are you at least going to eat breakfast?"

He was deflecting by focusing his nervous energy on me. I jogged into the kitchen, walked up behind him, wrapped my arms around his neck and kissed the side of his forehead. I reached over his shoulder and grabbed a corner of his toast, dipped it into the yolk of his poached egg and made a dramatic show of taking a bite.

"Mmmm, yummy," I said with a mouth full of food.

"I didn't mean my breakfast." He laughed. It was good to see him smile. I'd only been home for a few days, and he'd been consumed with stress.

Over the years, many real estate developers have approached my father about buying our resort. He'd always refused. Recently, a new development company called Wolfe Real Estate Holdings made him an offer six months ago. It didn't seem out of the ordinary at first. My father turned down the offer as he always did, but they refused to take no for an answer. He discovered that Wolfe Real Estate had been buying resorts all over the Caribbean, including two others in Barbados.

The offers persisted, and when my father threatened legal action, they stopped, except for one. The CEO of Wolfe Industries, of which the real estate company was a subsidiary, asked to meet with my father personally to discuss a deal. If my father refused after hearing his offer, it would be the end and Wolfe Industries would no longer pursue our resort. It seemed too good to be true because it had to be.

Before my father met my mother and retired to the quiet life of a resort owner in a tropical paradise, he was a corporate raider. He made millions of dollars looking for weak spots in companies, exploiting those weaknesses to take control in order to resell the company at a profit or dismantle it for parts. He'd seen this before because he'd done it before. This meeting *was* going to be the end. Wolfe Industries would no longer pursue The Sterling because they had no plans on losing the negotiations. Companies like Wolfe never took no for an answer. If they wanted our resort, they wouldn't stop until they got it.

This was why my father was so nervous. He knew how these things went, and the fact the CEO himself was handling negotiations wasn't a good sign.

He should've told me all of these things sooner, but he

didn't want to stress me out even more than I was at school. If he did, I probably would have skipped my summer internship to come home early. He was right. There was nothing I could do from Philly, but knowing my father was dealing with this stress on his own made me feel terrible. I gave him a big squeeze from behind.

"Relax, Dad. Everything's going to be fine." I kissed his cheek. "I'm here now." Then I turned to leave.

"Where are you going?" he called after me.

"Where do you think?" I laughed and called over my shoulder.

I stopped, turned and jogged over to the kitchen table, kissed my dad goodbye and ruffled his silver blonde hair before heading out the door.

WHEN I WAS A CHILD, my mother would take me to the beach as often as possible. She called it sea bathing, and to her, it was as crucial as taking vitamins and going to the gym would be to someone else. It always seemed silly until I went away to school. The constantly changing weather and the cold winters were terrible enough, but the lack of good beaches was almost unbearable.

Beginning in my freshman year, my father rented a house on the coast for the school year and hired a car and driver to take me to the Jersey shore whenever I wanted to stay. I went almost every weekend and still did when I was in school. Even when it was too cold to swim, I would sit on the beach wrapped in a blanket and watch the waves roll in for hours. It got me through my first year at Wharton when I thought about quitting constantly. As grateful as I was for the beaches in New Jersey, they couldn't hold a candle to the pink sand beaches back home.

I followed the path from our house to the main suites and headed for the elevator to the beach. The grounds of the resort are usually deserted this time of the morning, so I wasn't surprised when I didn't see anyone. The two towels Tianna, our head of housekeeping, always left for me next to the elevator were waiting when I pushed the button and waited.

"HEY, MIA HAMM," a deep rumbling voice called from above me.

I turned in the direction of the voice. The handsome man I saw yesterday playing football with his son was calling to me from the second-floor balcony.

"Who?"

"Mia Hamm. The famous soccer player."

"I know who Mia Hamm is. I'm not her, and you're in Barbados where we call it football."

"Well, I don't know your name. Why don't you tell me what it is so I know what to call you and then you can tell me where you learned to play *football* like that."

"I think you'll find that most people who grew up in the Caribbean can pass a football with some skill. I'm not special."

"I don't know if I agree with that." He grinned, and I felt myself flush. "And you still haven't told me your name."

"Where are your wife and son?" I asked, deciding to nip this little game in the bud.

His brow furrowed in confusion before realization hit.

"What? No. She is not my wife and Philip is not my son."

Something that felt suspiciously like hope caused my heart to flutter at his words, but he was probably lying.

"That little boy looked exactly like you."

"Hey, I'm not saying he's not a good looking kid." His grin returned, and so did my flush. "He's just not *my* kid."

"Well, his mother seemed interested. Why don't talk to her about *soccer*?"

"I'm not interested in his mother." He gave me a pointed look, his grin still firmly in place.

My stupid heart fluttered again.

"I'm already taken," he said.

The fluttering stopped.

"But the problem is, she won't tell me her name." He tucked his bottom lip between his teeth, still grinning.

And the fluttering returned. A deep breath helped me

calm myself and regain focus before I pressed the elevator button again, knowing that it would do nothing to make the elevator come faster.

I glared at him and rolled my eyes. He was leaning over his balcony waiting for an answer.

"No," I said finally.

"No, what?" he asked.

"Whatever you want. Whatever you think this is. The answer is no."

"It can be whatever you want it to be." That line would've been incredibly sleazy from anyone else, but he made it sound so sincere and almost convincing that it was clear I needed to keep my distance from him, no matter how charming he was and no matter how long it had been since I felt a man's hands on my body.

"Good," I said. Mercifully, the elevator arrived at that moment, and I stepped inside. "Nothing it is."

———

THE NEXT MORNING on my way to the elevator I saw the sexy footballer with the terrible pickup lines sitting on his balcony. His back was turned as I approached and he looked like he was working on a laptop, making me wonder if he was a writer traveling by himself looking for inspiration. I shook my head, determined not to let myself daydream about him any more than I've allowed myself since I laid eyes on him on that field. Those daydreams only intensified after our conversation yesterday and crept into last night's dreams. I needed to focus on surviving the walk to the elevator, wondering what he would say to me today and how I would respond.

I took a deep breath, squared my shoulders, lifted my chin and strolled down the path, past his balcony, and to the elevator. I grabbed my towels, pushed the button and waited. A few long silent minutes went by.

God, this is the slowest elevator known to man, I thought to myself as the seconds seemed to be cosplaying as minutes.

The man on the balcony still hadn't spoken. Maybe he was so involved in his work that he hadn't noticed me. Maybe he'd gone inside. It was for the best anyway. I told myself a long time ago that life was easier without *distractions* like him, but the curiosity was killing me, and that damned elevator still hadn't come.

Fuck it.

I took a deep breath and turned to the balcony. Not only was he still there, but as our eyes met, his smile grew into a wide, smug grin, but he didn't speak. He just smiled like the cat who caught the canary, and I was the canary in this scenario. He raised one questioning eyebrow. My breath caught in my throat and my face burned. I quickly turned around and began furiously jamming the elevator button with my finger.

The door finally slid open and I stepped inside and turned around. Apparently, I hadn't embarrassed myself enough because I couldn't stop my eyes from flicking upward at him.

He was still sitting there.

He was still looking at me.

And of course, he was still grinning the sexy grin.

My heart fluttered again.

Dammit.

FOUR

ALEXANDER

I woke up early, went to the gym, as usual, and returned to my suite and my perch on the balcony to wait for my mystery woman. She arrived on schedule, but this morning, she wasn't wearing the cover up she usually wore, only the bikini. The next decision I made was a reckless one.

I knew after my meeting with The Closer, my cover as an incognito guest would be blown. This woman haunted my dreams at night and invaded my every waking moment since I saw her on Saturday. My desire to close this deal was fading with each passing day and was being slowly replaced by a desire for her. Today would be my last chance, and I had a choice to make. I chose her.

Despite bounding down the steps barefoot and shirtless, I missed the elevator.

"Fuuuck," I gritted while pushing the call button for the

elevator and waiting for it to return. It took over ten minutes.

Once I buy this place the first thing I'm doing is replacing this elevator with a faster one, I thought to myself, checking my watch again.

By the time I made it to the beach, there was no sign of her.

Should I go back up the cliff or wait for her? I wondered. The possibility of searching for her crossed my mind for a split second, but how the hell would I explain that? If I went back to my suite, I could miss her again, and the meeting was just hours away. I couldn't risk it. No, I'd wait.

And that's exactly what I did.

FORTY-TWO MINUTES later I was sitting on the sand watching a crab ambling past my feet carrying a twig when I saw a small figure making their way to the elevator from the far side of the beach. It was her.

She walked slowly along the shoreline, her long curly hair was tousled by the breeze. As she got closer, something in her expression made me pause. She was never particularly cheerful, and I'd only seen her smile once, but today she looked decidedly sad. She should never wear that expression. She should always be wearing the smile I saw on the field on Saturday.

She stopped short when she saw me, and I jumped to my feet wiping the sand off of my hands and my shorts. Her expression hardened, and she continued towards the elevator. I stepped in behind her, and we both reached for the button with the arrow pointed up, briefly brushing our fingers together, sending a jolt of electricity up my arm and straight to my heart. Her eyes met mine, and I knew she'd felt it too. The elevator began its excruciatingly slow ascent up the cliff when I turned to face her.

"Hi." *Hi? Hi? Jesus fucking Christ, Alex.*

At any other moment I could've come up with the perfect way to start a conversation with her, but her beauty left me speechless.

Her skin was light brown and toasted golden by the sun. She had a perfect oval face with high chiseled cheeks smattered with brown freckles that stretched across the bridge of a gorgeous rounded nose that was the perfect landing pad for a kiss. Her lips were full, luscious and equally kissable. She surveyed me with pale gray eyes that were simultaneously fierce and sad. I moved closer as if some magnetic force was pulling me.

"Hi," she responded, and I could swear a corner of her mouth twitched, but the hint of a smile disappeared too quickly to be sure.

"Are you okay?" I took a step closer. She didn't move away and she tilted her head upwards to meet my steady gaze.

"I'm fine," she whispered, but it wasn't very convincing.

Cautiously, I reached out to caress her face. She leaned

into my touch and her eyelids fluttered closed as my palm slid across her cheek. Her fingertips glided over my chest and traced the tattoos on my arm leaving trails of heat that remained long after her fingertips grazed my skin. Every nerve ending in my body was responding to her touch and a few key blood vessels. I was trying desperately to focus all of my energy on her, but it was a struggle. She was easily the most beautiful woman I'd ever seen. Her skin was so warm and soft. Her scent was intoxicating. She smelled like a tropical summer breeze; sweet, salty, floral and fruity. My fingers found themselves nestled in her curls as I stroked her cheeks with my thumb.

"Can I hold you?" I whispered. It was all I wanted. Since the moment I laid eyes on her I felt this unexplainable desire to be near her. Seeing her sad and vulnerable like this fueled some primal instinct to want to wrap her in my arms and protect her, even if I had no idea why she needed protection.

She looked up at me, and her eyes searched my face for something. Whatever it was, she found it because she nodded and whispered one word, "please."

I pulled her close to me and wrapped one arm around her waist and the other around her back splaying my fingers and gently squeezing her into me. She sighed and melted against me before I felt her arms reach around my back pressing us even closer together. My heart was throwing myself against my ribcage as I pressed my nose into her neck to inhale her addictive scent.

"Kiss me," she whispered, and the sound was so faint I

broke our embrace and held her away from me so she could repeat it. "Kiss me."

"Are you sure? I didn't expect you to—"

"Please." Her whisper was a desperate plea, and I wasn't going to make her ask again. I slid my fingers back into her hair and tilted her head up as I slowly brought our lips closer. "Wait."

Shit. I knew this was too much. I should've waited, should've insisted on just holding her, I should've—

"You should stop the elevator," she whispered. I tilted my head and narrowed my eyes, slightly confused. "Behind you." She pointed her head towards the panel of buttons next to the doors.

I should've stopped the elevator. I was flooded with selfish relief as I reached behind myself and hit the red stop button on the elevator control panel, only taking my eyes off of her for the briefest moment.

The elevator jerked to a stop halfway between the cliff top and the beach.

"Are you sure about this?" I raised my eyebrows in expectation waiting patiently for her answer. I couldn't remember wanting anything as badly as what this woman asked of me, but I wasn't going to do it unless I knew she was one hundred percent sure.

"Yes," she nodded. "Make me forget…" Her eyes fluttered closed again, and I moved closer. Instead of going straight for her pillowy lips, I indulged myself by tenderly dragging my lips along her shoulder, across her throat, and over her cheek, gently trailing kisses along the way, blazing a trail of searing heat eliciting another contented sigh which I felt vibrating in her throat under my lips. She felt like heaven on earth.

When our lips finally met it was like an explosion. Her hands flew to the back of my head, and she dug her nails into my scalp pulling us closer together. My hands slid down her waist, and I cupped her ass and lifted her into my arms.

I pressed her body into the corner of the glass elevator with the Atlantic Ocean spread out behind us for miles. Her legs were also spread by the massiveness of my torso, and I pressed myself between her thighs. I was getting harder by the second. My hips slowly rocked back and forth, dragging my length up and down her throbbing sex, only separated by the thin fabric of my board shorts and her bikini bottoms. Her soft curves were writhing against me as I nibbled on her neck, ears, and shoulders causing her to make sexy little whimpering noises.

"I want to come," she moaned in my ear. "Make me come."

I could've come from hearing those words, but I steeled myself and focused on giving her what she wanted. This was about her, not about me. It was all about her.

"Yes, gorgeous." I pulled away from her immediately missing the feeling of her body pressed against mine as I began to trail kisses down her neck and chest. I freed one of her breasts from the triangle of her bikini top and took the entire areola my mouth and began to suck while circling and flicking the nipple with my tongue.

More contented moans spilled from her lips, and I wasn't sure how long I could last without relief. This wasn't a problem thinking about baseball could fix. I grunted in overwhelming frustration as my five senses were assaulted by this woman who was too good to be real, and I continued tasting her. I was licking and sucking on the softness of her stomach, her hips and finally stopped when I was facing her sex covered in the black Lycra fabric of her bikini. The scent of her arousal was enticing and my entire body burned with anticipation.

I looked up at her, and she stared back. The look of lust and longing in her eyes was mesmerizing. The thick dark lashes framing them make them stand out even more. They were hypnotizing, and she knew it.

"May I?" One side of my mouth quirked into a smile, and I raised an eyebrow.

She tucked her bottom lip between her teeth and nodded, giving me permission to continue my oral exploration of her body. I grinned before giving her a playful bite through her bikini bottoms, and her whole body twitched.

Fuck me.

I tugged the thin bows on the sides of her bottoms giving myself full access to the wetness between her thighs. I leaned in and inhaled deeply.

"Yes, gorgeous," I growled, feeling completely primal. "I'm gonna make you come right now." I leaned in again and with one smooth motion dragged my tongue through her outer lips, her inner lips, and once I curled the tip around her bud of pleasure, she came apart.

She made a noise I had never heard before. It was a cross between a grunt and a scream, and body-rocking paroxysms of pleasure accompanied it. I responded by steadying her thighs on my shoulders while licking and sucking every inch of her sex as she moaned and swore, gripping handfuls of my dark hair. I was intent on drowning her sadness in wave after wave of body numbing ecstasy, if only for a moment, but I was hoping to make it last as long as I could.

After what felt like a blissful eternity, her climax began to ebb and I was still devouring her like a starving man, encircling her entrance with my tongue consuming every drop of nectar she had to give me. I slowly rose trailing kisses up her waist, stomach, and breasts. I took her face in my hands and looked down at her.

"I need to be inside you." It was definitely a request, but phrased as a statement. This wasn't asking, it was begging. I've never been this turned on by anyone before. My body craved her. One taste was all it took to make me an addict. I wanted to bury myself in her warmth and die a thousand times in her arms. "Please," I added.

She tucked her bottom lip between her teeth again and nodded frantically in response before she grabbed the back of my head, pulling me into a fierce kiss. My hands roamed her body. I dug my fingers into the flesh behind her knees, pulling them up to wrap around my waist again. The scent of her arousal filled the air, fueling my desire as I reached for the zipper of my shorts.

A shrill beeping sound permeated our private bubble, and the real world came flooding in.

An alert on her watch was sounding. She broke our kiss and whipped her head around scanning the beach, possibly searching for any sign of people. It was still deserted which seemed to relieve her, but only slightly.

"I have to go." The sadness had returned to her face, but it was accompanied by fear and possibly regret.

Shit. I took a step forward.

"Do you *really* have to go?" I lowered my face to hers to kiss her, hoping my kiss could reassure her that in this elevator, with me, was exactly where she belonged.

"Yes," she hissed, "I do."

She jabbed the green button on the panel and the elevator hummed to life. She wrapped a towel around her naked hips and pressed herself into the corner nearest the elevator control panel and furthest away from me, her chest heaving. The elevator resumed its ascent with a small jerk.

I crossed the elevator car, wrapped my hands around her waist and looked down at her.

"Are you okay? I don't want you to get the wrong idea. This meant something to me, and I want—"

"Please don't finish that sentence. You don't have to. We're consenting adults. I'm just... You just caught me at a bad moment. This was a mistake."

"No," I shook my head. "It wasn't." I wrapped my arm tighter around her waist, bringing her closer to me. I lowered my face to hers, and she closed the distance, bringing our faces together and parting her lips for me, welcoming me into her mouth and tangling her fingers in my hair again.

"I'm sorry." She pulled away after a few moments. "I have to go." The look in her eyes told me that she didn't want to go and I didn't want her to go. I wanted to spend hours, days and weeks with her wrapped around me. After thirty-three years of doing everything that was expected of me under the watchful eyes of my grandfather and the world, I had spent fifteen minutes doing one reckless thing that had the potential to bring everything crashing down, and I didn't want to stop. The elevator doors opened at the clifftop revealing the path to the main houses. She scrambled to pick up her discarded bikini bottoms, but I was quicker.

"At least tell me your name."

"No." She shook her head firmly. "And don't tell me yours."

"Well, if this really didn't mean anything to you, then you should let me keep these as a souvenir." I held up the bottoms. She glanced at the scrap of black fabric in my hand then back at me just before the elevator door opened.

"You might as well," she called over her shoulder as she exited the elevator, clutching the towel more tightly around her waist and beginning to jog up the path toward what I assumed was her room. "Because this will never happen again."

FIVE

ALEXANDER

*T*hat didn't go according to plan. It was a stupid mistake, compounded by the fact that I was thrown entirely off my game.

No, not a mistake, but definitely stupid.

I hadn't stopped thinking about the mystery woman since meeting her, but I'd made the decision not to pursue her and try to keep my focus on the deal. She'd even told me she wasn't interested. She was full of shit, but she had given me another reason to keep my eyes on the ball.

This morning everything went out the window.

I was intent on getting her out of that elevator, into my bed and taking my time tasting every inch of that sweet little body. But fate had other plans. She left me standing there with a dick hard as a diamond and those tiny black bikini bottoms clenched in my fist. She said what happened in that elevator would never happen again. She was wrong. I would take care of my business with Sterling then dedicate the rest of my time in Barbados to finding her again.

I WAS SITTING on my balcony, poolside, clutching my little souvenir and replaying the delicious moments of an hour ago. I should have been preparing for the meeting, but I couldn't. I thought I was hooked when she was just a figure I watched walking to and from the elevator for the past two mornings. Now, she'd taken up permanent residence in my head, leaving no room for anything else. I didn't even hear Matt walk in.

"Hey, Dick. The door was open," he called from the sliding glass doors, scaring the shit out of me and almost causing me to drop the bottoms. "Why the fuck aren't you dressed?" He was the only person I employed who could talk me like that and the closest thing to a brother I would ever have.

"I don't think I can go. My heads not in the game."

"Not go?" He laughed incredulously. "You've been sucking Barnabas Sterling's metaphorical dick since undergrad. When you found out he owned this place; it was like a kid finding out Santa Claus was real."

I could hear his voice getting louder as he approached me and I stuffed the bottoms into my pocket.

"Now," he continued, bending over talking directly into my ear. "You're going to sack up, get your stinky ass in the shower, *clear your head* and get your shit together." He stood up and walked toward the door. Something about the way he said *clear your head* felt funny, but I ignored it. "Wheels up in thirty," he called from the kitchen. Matt started rummaging through the cabinets as I headed into the shower.

He was right. I need to clear my head, metaphorically and literally. My dick had been brick hard since the elevator, and there was no way I could go into an important negotiation like that. I stepped into the steamy cascade of water, leaned against the wall and closed my eyes. Her beautiful face contorted in ecstasy flooded my consciousness, and I began to stroke my dick.

With a handful of conditioner in my palm, I renewed my stroke, my hands slid up and down my length more easily as I imagined I was enveloped in her warm wetness.

"I want to come. Make me come."

That sweet voice whispered in my head as I licked my lips, still tasting her and quickening my stroke.

My release was like a cannon blast, and I grunted as I spent myself onto tiled walls of the shower. I struggled to catch my breath as I watched my wasted seed slide down the wall and snake around the drain until it disappeared.

I did feel more relaxed and ready for the meeting. I was Alexander Wolfe. I became one of the youngest CEOs of a Fortune 100 company at twenty-six. I could make this meeting my bitch, find my mystery woman and still have time for lunch.

Feeling energized, I emerged from the master suite

looking like my corporate alter ego: hair slicked back and clean-shaven in a perfectly tailored three-piece suit.

"Yeah, baby," Matt roared, "The Wolf is back." He handed me a mug of coffee, and I gulped it down. He slapped me on the back as we exited the suite.

Yeah, The Wolfe was back, but he also had a pair of black bikini bottoms in his suit pocket.

———

WE ARRIVED at the offices of Sterling's attorneys twenty minutes early. He could tell us no anywhere, but since he'd already threatened legal action, he wanted all negotiations to take place in front of legal counsel. His team was no doubt going to try to entrap us into saying something libelous and then use the threat of a lawsuit to convince us to stop pursuing The Sterling. It was brilliant, and it was what I would do, but it wasn't going to work.

Two members of our legal team walked in a minute before we did. The four of us approached the reception desk.

"Alexander Wolfe to see Barnabas Sterling."

"Yes, Mr. Sterling has been expecting you." She smiled. "He's been waiting for quite some time. Follow me, please." Another tactic. Some people think making your opponent wait gives you the upper hand and puts them on edge. The truth is, those who have real power don't play those kinds of games. The second party to the meeting was always late, even if they're twenty minutes early.

She led us down a corridor of glass-walled offices and conference rooms until we stopped at one where six people were seated at a long table.

Six. I laughed to myself.

The reception desk probably called ahead to say that we had four in our group and they scrambled to make sure they had more.

My breath caught as we approached the double glass doors. It was as though the air had been sucked from the room.

Sitting next to a much older, grayer and tanner Barnabas Sterling was the woman from the elevator.

Matt seemed just as taken aback as I was and he was probably thinking the same thing. If he said it out loud, I'd knock his teeth out, best friend or not.

"Alexander Wolfe, I presume." The Closer stood and extended his hand. "Barnabas Sterling and this is Cal…"

"Callie Sterling." She interrupted, but didn't extend her hand.

"Sterling?" I repeated, not entirely sure that I heard correctly.

"Yes," he replied. "She's my daughter."

Shit.

SIX

*A*lexander Wolfe.

My face flushed with a mixture of anger, embarrassment and, I hated to admit it, lust. It was him, and it was *him*. This morning's mystery encounter and the man threatening the future of my family's home were the same person.

I cursed myself for being so foolish. My father spent my whole life preparing me for this meeting with his tales of corporate espionage and tactics he would use to gain control of companies. Dad's tales made him sound like a James Bond, without the drinking and sex, which I'm sure he just omitted for my benefit. He enjoyed reliving his glory days, and I hung on his every word. I couldn't wait to grow up, attend Wharton and take the corporate world by storm, just like he did. Based on this morning's encounter, I was off to a shitty start.

Something like this should have been expected. In all my research for the meeting, I couldn't find one photo of Alexander Wolfe. It made sense. My father said it was always better to keep yourself as mysterious as possible. The less your enemy knew about you, the less ammunition they had to use against you. It was one of the reasons I didn't have any social media accounts. That and I spent all my time studying and reading, not doing anything remotely Instagram worthy.

Alexander Wolfe used his anonymity to gain access to The Sterling and gather information. In the process, he gathered me. It hurt deeply that the most intimate and erotic moment in my life had been a lie, and I allowed it to happen because he'd caught me at a vulnerable moment. I was also grateful that I was able to stop myself before things went too far. The fury I felt galvanized me. I would not be making any more mistakes where Alexander Wolfe was concerned. If he thought this morning's encounter was going to throw me off my game, he was going to learn that I wasn't a Sterling in name only.

"YES," I replied curtly, "I'm his daughter. May we resume the meeting?"

"But you're so," he was mumbling under his breath, but I heard the sound of a "b" in the offing.

"Black," I said matter-of-factly. "Well spotted, Mr. Wolfe." I often got this type of reaction when I was out with Dad.

I'd been mistaken for his girlfriend or mistress more times than I could count. It made him furious, but I always thought it was funny. I got a big kick out of calling him Daddy in public and watching people squirm uncomfortably.

"No!" Mr. Wolfe almost shouted. "I wasn't going to say that at all," he continued, stammering. "I was going to say… beautiful." His mouth snapped shut, and it was obvious that he couldn't believe what he'd just said. Judging by the looks on everyone else's faces, they couldn't believe it either. My father's face grew stern. His eyes narrowed into slits and he leaned forward—clearly not amused. The man sitting next to Mr. Wolfe wasn't amused either. He also narrowed his eyes at him and gave him a confused, angry look.

I found myself slightly flushing at his declaration, and I was getting the feeling that maybe Alexander Wolfe *didn't* know who I was when we met in the elevator. It tickled me that I might have had the upper hand after all. I decided to twist the knife.

"Okay." I began. "We've established that I'm the daughter of Barnabas Sterling, I'm Black and, apparently, I'm also beautiful. Are we all caught up?" I looked around the room for effect, finally locking eyes with Alexander Wolfe himself and raising my eyebrows. He didn't respond as I knew he wouldn't. Our legal team was stifling smiles, and one of the opposing counsel coughed loudly to mask a titter of laughter.

"Wonderful." I paused for dramatic effect. "We're gathered

here to satisfy an agreement. If one Barnabas Sterling," I patted Dad's hand, "agreed to meet in person with one Alexander Wolfe, then Wolfe Industries would abandon all pursuit of ownership of the property, The Sterling Beachfront Paradise and Resort, henceforth during these negotiations to be referred to as The Sterling. Are all parties in agreement with the terms of this meeting?" I scanned the room before settling on Mr. Wolfe's face. He was staring at me as though I'd grown two heads. Finally, the pale blonde man sitting next to him nudged him which caused him to nod.

"We'll need a verbal confirmation, Mr. Wolfe." I smiled at him.

He cleared his throat. "Yeah. Yes." He nodded again. The blonde man shook his head, his lips forming a thin tight line.

"Great, let the record show that all parties are in agreement." I nodded again. "Mr. Wolfe, we're listening." I interlaced my fingers on the desk, tilted my head and jutted my chin forward in the universal *I'm listening* pose. He was still staring at me dumbfounded. The man sitting next to him that I now recognized as Matthew Widnicki, the head of the real estate division of Wolfe Industries, leaned forward, clearly annoyed by Wolfe's bizarre behavior.

"We're prepared to offer you twenty percent above the last offer with three years occupancy. During those three years, you will retain full rights as well as fifty percent of the profits."

Our faces remained impassive.

"And," he added quickly, "we will retain all of The Sterling's staff during the transition. You're not going to get a better deal than that. That's it. That's our final offer." He leaned back in his chair.

Dad and I turned to face each other. He gave me a small smile. I returned it. We turned to Mr. Widnicki with our game faces.

"We are rejecting that offer. Thanks for coming in, gentlemen." I gave them a warm, closed mouth smile. "Travel safe."

"What?" Mr. Widnicki said, his voice seething with anger. "That's it?"

"I believe we've satisfied the terms of the agreement."

"That agreement wasn't in writing," he countered. Matthew's face, while pale compared to Alex's tanned cast when the meeting began, was reddening with every passing second.

"You're right. It wasn't." I whipped a file out of my portfolio and tossed it across the table along with a small black zip drive. "It was a verbal agreement entered into by my father's personal secretary, Susan Jones and a…" I paused scanning my copy, "Margaret Watson, acting on behalf of your corporation. That's the full transcript and an audio recording. I'm sure I don't have to tell you that it is legal and binding. I should also remind you that I reiterated the conditions of the meeting and Mr. Wolfe agreed. Shall I have the stenographer read them back to you?"

I indicated a person sitting in the corner in front of a small black stenotype. Mr. Widnicki looked at them in mild shock as if they'd just appeared in a puff of smoke.

"If you continue to pursue ownership of The Sterling, we would have to add breach of contract in addition to harassment." I took a deep breath and pushed myself up from my chair. "If there's nothing else, I think this meeting has officially ended. I'll leave you the room."

I quickly gathered my things and walked out. Dad and our lawyers were following closely behind. Alexander Wolfe's eyes burned holes in me as I forced myself to take slow, deliberate steps because if I dared to look at him, I was sure I'd fall over. We turned the corner and entered the office of Dad's lead counsel. As soon as I heard the lock click, I began shaking from the adrenaline and sucking in deep breaths.

"Bug!" Dad cried. "That was amazing!" Only my dad could use my childhood pet name to praise me for doing the most adult thing I'd ever done.

"It was?" My voice was shaking. "Do you think it worked? Is it over?"

"Probably not," he said, "but you gave them one hell of a run for their money. You definitely bought us some time." He kissed my forehead. "C'mon, let's go get some ice cream."

I smiled. I'd just gone toe to toe with one of the most

successful CEOs in the world and won, but my dad wanted to reward me the same way he did when I won my primary school talent show.

"I'd like to take a rain check, Dad. I'm just too wound up, and I want to get rid of this nervous energy."

"I know that feeling." He smiled sadly. "First you love it, then you hate it. So, enjoy it now. I'll see you at home."

Everyone filed out of the office one by one leaving me alone with my thoughts.

This day had been crazy, and I finally felt like I could relax. I couldn't believe how exciting that was. Dad always said, when you had them on the ropes keep punching, and I kept punching. I took a deep breath, and my thoughts drifted to Alexander Wolfe.

Once I got over the initial shock of seeing him again, I had to admit he looked sexy as hell in the meeting. His facial hair was gone making him look like a handsome superhero as he strode down the corridor. He was wearing a dark blue suit that could've only been made for him. The rippling muscles that I knew resided underneath were barely restrained. The pale blue cuffs extended past his jacket sleeves displaying the simple polished platinum cufflinks and watch. I could see hints of his arm tattoos peeking from under his watch band. This Alexander Wolfe may have looked different, but the man who set my body on fire this morning was still there.

My mind drifted to this morning. I could still feel his hands on me and taste myself on his lips. The ghost of his kisses traveling down my body made my flesh tingle, and

I felt myself aching for a release. I took a deep breath and began to gather my things to leave the office. The day had been a confusing day of firsts, and I desperately needed to go somewhere to make sense of it all.

I opened the door to leave and found myself face to face, or actually face to chest, with Alexander Wolfe.

SEVEN

CALYPSO

*A*s my eyes slowly rose to meet his, my breath caught in my throat. He was still as gorgeous up close as he was in the elevator, but his face was twisted in a look of fury.

I dropped my portfolio and backed into the office in terror. He followed me in, locking the door behind him. What must have been the small sound of the lock clicking seemed deafening as I started to panic internally, doing my best to keep my face impassive as possible, while I scanned the office for a potential weapon. I briefly considered a stapler, a cup of newly sharpened pencils and a silver picture frame before settling on a large wireless keyboard. I set my face, glaring at him and holding it aloft like a cricket bat, ready to strike.

His entire body softened as his fury changed to shock then his face melted into laughter, displaying a matching set of deep dimples, because of course, he had to have dimples on top of every other sexy thing.

"Callie," he chuckled. "What are you planning to do with that?"

"Take one step closer and find out," I threatened. I realized how foolish I must have looked and wondered if the pencils would have been a better option.

"Could you put that down, please?" He was still trying to stifle laughter. "I would never hurt you, ever." He sounded so sincere, I began to lower the keyboard. "I just want to talk."

Of course, this was another tactic. He was trying to use me again to get his hands on The Sterling and maybe me in the process. I wouldn't mind the latter, but I meant what I said about no more mistakes regarding this man. I raised the keyboard higher.

"I believe we did all the talking we're going to do in the meeting, Mr. Wolfe." I gulped and tried to maintain my resolve, but the look on his face was chipping it away.

"Mr. Wolfe?" He had the nerve to look offended. "I'm Mr. Wolfe, after this morning?" He tried to take a step toward me reaching out his hands. I raised the keyboard higher, and he backed away.

"Do you mean, this morning when I almost had mind-blowing elevator sex with a complete stranger who was only using me to get his greedy hands on my parents' resort?" I was apparently losing control of the situation because I did not mean to blurt out the word *mind-blowing*. He didn't seem surprised to hear it, however. He just smiled the smug smile I recognized from the balcony yesterday.

"I promise you." He was almost pleading and holding his hands up, but not daring to step forward. "I had no idea who you were. You were a gorgeous stranger who walked by my balcony every morning. I swear I only wanted to talk to you but…" His voice died away, and I knew he was thinking about the elevator because I was thinking about the elevator.

"And I'm supposed to believe you just happened to be at The Sterling on the morning of the meeting, people-watching from your balcony?" I asked, raising an eyebrow.

"No," he said. "I was definitely there doing recon, trying to gather information that could help with negotiations—"

"Ha! I knew it—"

"I wanted to know what was so special about the place and understand why someone like your father would hold onto it like this."

"Did it ever occur to you that it's not your business to know why my father does what he does and just take no for an answer?"

"No." He laughed again. "That thought would have never occurred to me. There's a reason for everything. Help me."

Now, it was my turn to laugh.

"Help you?"

"Help me understand why your father is so stuck on this place. Help me satisfy my curiosity, and I'll back off. I promise."

"You already did that," I said, "with a legally enforceable verbal agreement. Don't you remember?"

"Come on, Callie. You and I both know my lawyers can rip that to shreds," he said. My dad was right. The victorious high I was feeling was being slowly replaced by dread. "If anything, you bought yourself some time. I guess you really are The Closer's daughter." The compliment made my chest swell, but I pushed away the sentiment.

"You want me to help you by giving you information that you could use to hurt my father," I began, addressing him as if he were toddler, "and in exchange you will give me your word that you'll stop pursuing the sale, which you've already done in front of a half a dozen lawyers, which you just told me in the same breath meant nothing. Did I miss anything?"

"Okay." He put his hands up again. "When you say it that way it sounds bad." He smirked, and I rolled my eyes. "Look, Callie, I don't know how to do this. I only know I haven't been able to think about anything else but you since this morning. Fuck, since I saw you on that field. I want to spend some time with you, get to know you. Just give me a few hours." He looked like a puppy waiting for a treat. His sparkling blue eyes chipped away at the final bit of anger I had left. I slowly lowered the keyboard to the desk.

"Fifteen minutes," I said, trying to flex the soreness out of my biceps. He narrowed his eyes with a sexy smirk.

"Four hours." He countered.

"Forty-five minutes."

"Two."

"One."

"Okay." He conceded. "One hour."

"No elevators." Then I added quickly, "and I'm not going to your suite. In fact, I won't meet you at The Sterling."

"I will meet you anywhere you want, anytime."

I exhaled a deep sigh and scribbled on a post-it note with one of the pencils that almost became a weapon, while seriously questioning my sanity.

He took the folded paper from my hand, using the opportunity to brush my fingertips with his, sending a familiar tingling to my spine before radiating to every inch of my body.

His eyebrows furrowed as he opened the slip of paper and read it. "This is in three days." He looked at me. I crossed my arms and shrugged, silently asking him if there was a problem. His lips formed a tight line, and he read the note again. "You didn't write down your phone number."

"You didn't ask for my phone number."

"Could you write down your phone number?" He held out the slip of paper. "Please."

"No." I gave my head a small shake without breaking eye contact. His eyes narrowed, but I saw the ghost of a smile haunting the gorgeous mouth that had become so well acquainted with my body this morning.

"What if I have to cancel or reschedule?" He grinned at me.

"Don't cancel. Don't reschedule." I dropped my arms and leaned back on the desk, unintentionally arching my back. His eyes flickered to my breasts.

"What if I'm running late?"

"I wouldn't even think about being late, if I were you."

"You're not budging on this number thing, are you?" He took a step closer, and I shook my head.

"I'm trying to keep my monumental lapses in judgment to two for the day."

"Two?"

"The elevator and…" I nodded my head towards the folded sheet of paper tucked between his index and middle fingers.

He grinned and took a step closer. "I think you'll change your mind about both of those." The scent of his soap and cologne were faint and did nothing to mask the smell of the man I was wrapped around this morning. I was almost overtaken by the urge to sweep everything off of the desk behind me, grab the lapels of his suit jacket and pull him on top of me. Instead, I cleared my throat, reached past him and opened the door to the office.

"See you in three days, Mr. Wolfe."

"Alex." He corrected with that sexy dimpled smile of his.

"See you in three days, Mr. … Alex."

He smiled and backed out the office keeping me in view before turning and striding towards the elevator. When he reached it, he turned around to see if I was still watching him and I was. He stepped inside, and the last thing I saw was his gorgeous grin as doors slid closed.

Alexander Wolfe.

Shit.

EIGHT

ALEXANDER

*S*he was Barnabas Sterling's daughter.

I couldn't fucking believe it. How could anyone that beautiful come from that guy? Not that he was a bad looking guy, but Callie was fucking gorgeous.

I'd been waiting my entire adult life to sit face to face with The Closer, and when the opportunity arrived, I was hypnotized by his daughter.

The sexy, uninhibited enchantress I encountered in the elevator this morning was replaced with a sharply dressed corporate warrior. She was wearing makeup, but not much. Her freckles were still visible, and it made my cock twitch remembering the first time I saw them stretched across the smooth, perfect skin of her nose and cheeks. Her hair was pulled back into a tight French braid that extended halfway down her back. Her gorgeous body was encased in a form-fitting combination of a short sleeve white button down blouse and tight black pencil skirt.

The family resemblance became more evident once the meeting began. The Sterlings couldn't be more different at first glance, but side by side I noticed they had the same posture and many of the same mannerisms. Callie's steel gray eyes which were filled with desire when I last saw them were now cold, calculating and menacing. I immediately recognized them from Sterling's old headshot.

But when Callie opened her mouth, the resemblance was undeniable. The meeting was over before it began. She was cool, calm and cutthroat. Her beauty was disarming, and she took advantage. It was like jumping into a pool expecting to swim with dolphins and finding a couple of great white sharks circling you with their rows of teeth bared. I was a complete mess, but getting my ass kicked in a negotiation never felt so good. Matt at least tried to salvage the meeting, but I knew it was no use. We were beaten. They never had any intention of considering our offer. Their only objective was getting us to back off.

The meeting ended abruptly with Callie and her team striding off victoriously leaving us stunned in the conference room wondering what the fuck happened. The look of abject triumph on her face made me want to rip her out of that pencil skirt, bend her over the conference table, pull on that braid and bury myself in that sweet pussy until she made all the noises she made this morning.

Our lawyers left the room next, probably reading Matt's expression and wanting to stay clear of the impending explosion. Instead, Matt pounded the table with his fist, got up and stalked out of the office. We'd had bad days before, he'd be fine.

I was left in the conference room alone with more questions, and only one person had the answers.

A few moments later I saw Barnabas Sterling walking down the hallway with two of his lawyers. I guessed the other two went back to the mailroom, the intern pool or wherever they fished them out of at the last minute. We locked eyes for a brief moment, and his face hardened as he passed. He was definitely not a fan, but I also noticed Callie wasn't with them.

I jumped from my chair and exited the conference room and headed in the opposite direction. There was one office at the end of the corridor, and the door was closed. I was ready to knock when a thought popped into my head.

What if she knew?

What if the sweet, sexy, and innocent act was a ploy to throw me off my game for the meeting? Was it a coincidence that my suite was in direct view of the elevator she walked past every day? Why wasn't she wearing a cover-up today of all days? It worked like a fucking charm. She played me, and I blew my chance with The Closer. I started feeling the anger rise until the door opened.

She was looking up at me her eyes wide and her jaw agape, then something in my face made her back away. Fear.

In an instant she was backed into the corner of the office, holding up a keyboard ready to defend herself. In hindsight, locking the door was a bad decision. I only did it because I didn't want us to be interrupted but I understood the implication. The sight of the ferocity in her face juxtaposed with the futility of her chosen weapon was hilarious, and I couldn't help but laugh. She might have been better off with the cup of pencils.

I accomplished my goal of finding my mystery woman before lunch and I somehow managed to convince her to see me again, so the meeting wasn't a total waste.

I left the room knowing three things: she was as clueless about my identity this morning as I was about her's, she was as smart as she was sexy and for the first time in my life, work had become the second most important thing on my mind.

———

Matt avoided me for the rest of the day. He had a hell of a temper, and I did too, but this time he was right. That meeting was a fucking disaster, and it was my fault, but for some reason, I didn't care.

That was bullshit.

Callie was the reason I didn't care. Our encounter in the elevator was the hottest and most reckless thing I'd ever done. There were no regrets, but it was probably good that she put a stop to it when she did. I didn't even have a condom, and I was pretty sure that bikini didn't have any pockets. What was my plan? Pull out? Plan B? Did they have Plan B in Barbados? Would I fuck the shit out of her and spend the next two weeks praying that she wasn't pregnant, didn't have a disease or wasn't bat shit crazy?

It was clear I was obsessed with her body, but her brain? Holy fuck. I could spend hours with my hand wrapped around my dick, reliving the look on her face when she threw that folder on the conference table. When I found her in that office, she went from being fully prepared to beat the shit out of me with a keyboard to having me wrapped around her finger.

Which one was more of a turn on? Fuck if I knew.

I'd never been spoken to like that, never been denied a request with so much confidence. Even her body language spoke volumes. She leaned back on the desk, head held high, shoulders relaxed, and chest bared. All her fear was gone. She knew she wasn't in danger from me because she was in control. I didn't know whether or not to grab her and kiss her senseless or fall to my knees and worship her.

———

I WOKE up earlier than usual. I shouldn't say, woke up because a better choice of words would have been gotten out of bed, because I didn't get a lot of sleep. I decided to head to the gym as soon as they opened so I could be back in time to catch Callie on her way to the beach—if she decided to go to the beach today.

I was sitting on my balcony arms folded over each other, my chin resting on my forearms watching the path leading to the elevators. My phone was sitting on my lap, buzzing and pinging with the two dozen emails I usually got first thing in the morning after Maggie filtered out the bullshit. My hand didn't have its usual Pavlovian response to the alerts, and all my focus was on the path. I was starting to think she'd decided to forego the beach or take another path to avoid me.

She strode up the path looking every bit as gorgeous as she always did but more so because the sight of her sent signals to my other four senses. My brain was flooded with memories of her addictive taste, her intoxicating scent, the sexy moans that filled my ears and the softness of her skin under my fingertips. She was wearing a gold bikini today, and it almost blended in with her complexion giving the illusion that she was wearing nothing at all. She was also wearing a cover-up, and it was one I'd never seen before. It was long, black and incredibly sheer, further fueling the illusion of nudity. Our eyes locked briefly when she looked up at the balcony as she passed. Her stride didn't break as she continued towards the elevator. The hint of a smile, or what I hoped was a smile, sparked that same reckless feeling that found me bounding down the stairs yesterday, and before I could stop myself, I was running down the path calling her name.

"Can I help you, Mr. Alex?" She spun to face me.

"Where are you going?"

Jesus Christ. Did I just ask that?

"The beach, but I think you already know that." She tilted her head.

"I'll come with you."

"I'd rather go to the beach alone." Concern clouded her

face, and I wondered if she was worried about the prospect of sharing an elevator with me again.

"I promise to keep my hands and lips to myself." I held my hands up. "But I won't hold you to the same standards." I smirked, hoping for a similar response, but her face remained impassive.

"Thank you. But if it's all the same, I'd still prefer to go alone."

"Well, you know, there are no private beaches in Barbados. So, technically you couldn't stop a guest of The Sterling who happens to want to go to the beach at the same time you do."

"Does your brain have an off switch or is everything open for negotiation?"

"I could ask you the same question," I replied causing the corners of her full, soft lips to quirk into a small smile. A warm feeling spread through my chest causing it to expand. She was struggling to suppress that smile, the smile I gave her, and it made me want to work even harder to bring it back.

"Fine. What can I say to make you go away so I can enjoy the beach in peace?"

"Ten digits, but I'll settle for the last seven. I'm assuming the first three are 246?" I raised a hopeful eyebrow. She rolled her eyes and shook her head. "Then have breakfast with me."

"How do you know I haven't already had breakfast?"

"Then call it second-breakfast."

Her lips twitched again. A second smile. A little bit bigger than the last.

"If I have *second-breakfast* with you then I'll spoil *elevenses*." Her face was serious, but she just made a Tolkien crack. *Fuck me.* The goofy, friendless, teenage nerd that I'd spent years exercising, working and fucking away sat up, pushed his glasses up his nose and tilted his head in curiosity.

"Is that a no?" I asked when I regained the power of speech. Her response was a shake of the head causing her long mane of curly hair to swing side to side before she swiped the towels off of the table and walked to the elevator. I followed her, but I wasn't sure I'd meant to. She whipped around to face me.

"I said I wanted to go to the beach alone and you need to respect that." Her eyes were fierce. "Do other women respond positively to all this pestering?"

Pestering?

I thought I was flirting. To be honest, I've never *pestered* anyone. When I was a kid, I was too terrified to *pester* girls, especially ones that looked like Callie. Once I became *Alexander Wolfe, CEO,* I never had to.

"Shit. I'm sorry." I said taking a few steps back while rubbing the back of my neck which had suddenly grown hot. "You're absolutely right. I didn't mean to make you uncomfortable. Enjoy the beach. I hope I haven't fucked this up. We're still on for Friday, right?"

She didn't smile, but her expression softened. The elevator doors slid open at that moment, and she stepped inside and turned to face me.

"Two eggs: over light, whole wheat toast: lightly buttered, black tea and a bowl of fresh fruit. I'll be sitting there—" She pointed to the bistro table closest to the elevator. "—at eight-thirty. Please be on time."

As the elevator doors closed, her eyes cut away from mine, and her face spread with a dazzling grin. I earned a fucking grin.

Fuck me.

NINE

CALYPSO

*T*oday turned out to be a good day to go to the beach, and I took it as a positive omen for my impromptu breakfast with Alexander Wolfe. I knew I should be more cautious, but I was inexplicably drawn to him.

I stepped into the elevator and pushed the up arrow, bracing myself for what, I wasn't sure.

The doors opened, and Alexander Wolfe was sitting at the table I'd indicated reading *The Wall Street Journal,* holding a mug, and the familiar smell of coffee grew stronger as I approached the table. There were two settings, and I could see my breakfast, or my second-breakfast, laid out as I'd requested. Steam rose from the teapot. I looked at my watch. It was 8:15.

"There she is." He stood, grinning, as I approached the table and walked around to pull out my chair.

"That's not necessary." I reached for the chair, but again, he was faster.

"Please," he said and gestured towards the empty seat. I sighed and sat as he pushed the chair under me.

"Thank you." I pulled my hair into a ponytail and lifted the lid on my plate. The food was still hot. "How long has this been here?"

"A few minutes."

"How did you know when I was coming up the cliff?" I poured myself a cup of tea and sipped.

"I didn't. I've been ordering your breakfast every fifteen minutes."

I almost choked on my tea. "What?" I asked after clearing my throat. "How many breakfasts does this one make?" I pointed at my plate with a triangle of toast before using it to break the yolk of one of my eggs.

"Three. Which reminds me…" He grabbed his cell phone and tapped the screen with his thumb. "Yes, this is Mr. Underhill." He paused, smiling. I rolled my eyes and shook my head at him. "She's here. Thank you." He glanced at me. Another pause. "I will… fifty percent. Thank you again." When he ended the call, he smiled at me. "Desmond says good morning and he hopes you enjoy your breakfast."

"You told him you were having breakfast with me?" I asked, suddenly tense.

"No, I told him your order and he knew it was for you."

Desmond was our room service manager. He'd known me since I was a little girl. I checked the order of fresh fruit and noticed the absence of cantaloupe and abundance of blueberries, meaning he definitely knew the breakfast was for me and he wanted me to know that he knew. I wondered how quickly this news would get back to my father.

"Mr. Underhill?" I raised an eyebrow. "Really?"

The sheepish smile that followed my question made him look younger somehow. "I couldn't exactly check in under my real name, could I? I have a question for you." He placed his folded paper on the table and leaned forward reaching for my hand. "Why haven't I seen you before this week?"

I placed one hand in my lap and used the other to reach for a blueberry. "I'm home from school for the summer."

"School?" he repeated. His tan face paled, and he withdrew his hand slightly.

"Yes." I smiled sweetly, enjoying watching him squirm momentarily. "School."

He wiped his hand over his face and leaned back in his chair. After a few deep breaths, he asked, "So, how old are—"

"I've just completed the second year of my MBA program at Wharton." I smiled again. "I'm twenty-three." Alexander Wolfe aka Mr. Underhill had been tortured enough, though I would've paid good money to know what was running through his mind for those two minutes.

"Wharton, huh?" The color returned to his face, and the corners of his mouth quirked mischievously, suggesting that I may not be completely off the hook for teasing him. "Your dad's old stomping grounds."

"Yes. I've never wanted to go anywhere else."

"Harvard has a pretty good MBA program." He replied with a wink.

"Really?" I tilted my head and grinned. "Is that where you learned those amazing negotiating skills I witnessed yesterday?"

His face split into a wide grin that gave way to a deep belly laugh and soon I was laughing just as hard. It took a long time to gain our composure.

Alex finally sighed, wiping tears of laughter from his eyes and said, "No. No amount of lectures could have prepared me for yesterday. Any part of yesterday." His eyes met mine triggering a full body flush culminating in a grand finale that caused the muscles between my thighs to clench.

"So, do you always read the paper?" My segue was clumsy, but I had to say something to take our minds off of how close we were to the elevator and his suite and how easy it would be to slip into either one to pick up where we left off yesterday.

"Every morning. Don't you?"

"I do, but most people read the paper on tablets. I'm always surprised when I see someone else still reading the paper on *paper*."

"I guess, I'm old fashioned, but it reminds me of my grandfather. He had a favorite armchair he would sit in every morning, drink coffee and read the paper. Reading the newspaper on tablets always feels weird to me. Great for sharing articles, but..." He shrugged.

"Same. My dad reads the Journal every morning. When I was little, I used to wait until he was done and sneak it into my room to read it. One morning, I think I was about nine or ten, I opened the paper on my bed and Dad had circled articles that he thought I should read with little notes like, *'I predicted this would happen ten years ago'* or *'Pay attention, Bug. This is how you run a company into the ground.'* He still does it sometimes." I smiled at the memory and looked up to meet Alex's eyes.

He was gazing at me with a funny expression that I couldn't place. It made butterflies flutter in my tummy while simultaneously filling me with dread. Spending time with Alexander Wolfe was easy and moving into territory beyond physical attraction. I had to force myself to remember that this man was also actively trying to ruin my life. This would be a lot easier if he wasn't so charming.

"Hey, you okay? You went away for a second." His expression changed to one of concern.

"I'm fine, but I should go." My chair made a scraping sound as I abruptly stood. "Thank you for breakfast."

"Calypso."

"Hey, Dad," I said trying to keep my voice light and breezy. There was no way he didn't know about my *second-breakfast,* and if he knew the guest who ordered my breakfast three times, checked in with the name Mr. Underhill, he would know exactly who my dining companion was.

How many times had Dad read The Hobbit *and* The Lord of Rings *trilogy to me before bedtime?*

"How was the beach?"

I placed my hands on his shoulders and stood on tip-toes to kiss his cheek. "Today is definitely a good day to go to the beach." I grinned and waggled my eyebrows, making him blush slightly. Hopefully, he would be distracted thinking about his own trip to the beach this afternoon, but it wasn't enough to derail his line of questioning.

"How was breakfast?" He looked down at me with his eyebrows raised. My heart began to pound so, I turned to walk towards the stairs to my bedroom.

"It wasn't planned, Dad. We just kind of, bumped into each other." That was a poor choice of words, and I was glad he couldn't see my face.

"Be careful, bug. We have no idea what he's after. I rang Tianna earlier. *Mr. John R. Underhill* was scheduled to check out this morning, but as of yesterday afternoon has decided to extend his stay by a month. Why do you suppose that is?"

My stomach flipped thinking it might be because of our date on Friday.

Shit, I just called it a date.

Alex was disappointed that I didn't make it for the same day. I just assumed he was being impatient. Was it possible that he changed his plans just for me?

"I don't know." I shrugged. "He has other properties on the island. Maybe he's just comfortable here. This is a five-star resort, Dad." I turned and grinned at him.

"Very funny, young lady," he said, but he wasn't smiling. "Keep your wits about you. We won the battle yesterday, but I have a feeling the war isn't over."

I nodded seriously and climbed the stairs.

THE NEXT MORNING, I waved to Alex on the way to the beach, and when I stepped off of the elevator forty-five minutes later, he was waiting at our table.

"What number breakfast is this?" I asked when I sat down. He insisted on pulling my chair out again. This time I didn't argue.

"Two," he replied with a self-satisfied grin. "Either I'm getting better, or maybe you didn't spend as much time at the beach as you did yesterday."

I shrugged. Today was definitely a shorter beach day, but I didn't want to dwell on it.

"What's this?" I said to change the subject. There was a rolled up newspaper next to my plate.

"Well, I figured maybe you'd want your very own Journal, so you wouldn't have to steal one from your old man." He folded his own paper and placed it beside his coffee in order to catch my reaction.

"I'm perfectly capable of getting my own paper, but this was very thoughtful. Thank you." He'd made me giggle, and it felt good to laugh.

"How was the beach?" he asked.

I felt my face fall slightly, but I forced a smile.

"Fine. How was your work out?"

His eyes narrowed slightly, but he didn't press any further.

"Fine." He nodded thoughtfully. "Hey, um, I wanted you to know...about Tuesday..."

"What about Tuesday?" He must have been talking about the elevator, but Tuesday had been a very busy day for both of us.

"I wanted you to know that I've never done anything like that before."

"Mr. Wolfe," I grinned, "are you telling me you're a virgin?"

He did his grin to belly laugh combo from yesterday. Something told me he didn't laugh like this often. It seemed to take him by surprise.

"Definitely not, but something about you affects my ability to think rationally..." He seemed to lose his train of thought then regained focus. "I didn't want you to think that was the sort of thing I did all the time or ever." His face was completely serious, and I knew he was trying to read my expression. He seemed too honest and sincere to not be completely full of shit, but the fucking butterflies returned to my stomach, and they were buying every word.

"Well," I swallowed and continued. "I know this is the point where I'm supposed to say the same thing, but the truth is that our reservations department has strict instructions to book all tall, handsome men in that suite so I can ravage them in that elevator."

More belly laughter erupted from Alex.

"So you think I'm handsome?" he asked with a sexy grin. The butterflies were now hummingbirds.

"Is that all you got from that?" I crossed my legs and squeezed my thighs together in an effort to tether myself to reality.

He shrugged. "So?" His raised eyebrow was waiting for a response.

"Yes, Alexander Wolfe. You are very handsome, but I don't think you need me to tell you that."

"I disagree. I didn't know I needed anything more than I needed you to tell me how handsome you think I am."

Despite my best effort, I started chuckling, and I couldn't stop. He'd somehow managed to turn my entire morning around without even knowing I needed it.

"I should go." Now. I should have left ten minutes ago. I shouldn't have been sitting here in the first place.

"Breakfast tomorrow?" he asked. I wasn't sure I could stomach two bad days in a row.

"We'll see," I smiled. "But I'll definitely see you tomorrow." I opened the check presenter, took the pen and scribbled on the back of the receipt.

"What's this?" he asked craning his neck.

"My phone number," I met his eye, "unless you've changed your mind and you don't want it anymore."

"No. I haven't changed my mind." He grabbed the small black leather folder as if he were afraid I would change *my* mind.

"That's for emergencies. You know, in case you need to cancel or reschedule."

"Not a chance."

WHEN I GOT HOME ten minutes later, there was a text message on my phone. He must have sent it as soon as I walked away from him at breakfast.

UNKNOWN: I NEVER GOT TO TELL YOU HOW MUCH I LIKED YOUR NEW BIKINI. I'M NOT TOO CRAZY ABOUT THE DRESS THING YOU'RE WEARING OVER IT, BUT YOU MAKE ANYTHING LOOK GOOD.

After flopping on my bed and staring at the message for a few minutes, I saved Alex's number and typed a response.

ME: I COULDN'T FIND MY COVER UP ON TUESDAY, AND THE SAME DAY SOMEONE STOLE HALF OF MY BIKINI. SO, I NEEDED TO DO A LITTLE SHOPPING.

He replied seconds later.

MR. UNDERHILL: I CAN'T PRETEND I'M SORRY ABOUT YOUR MISSING COVER UP, BUT SINCE I'M THE SOMEONE WHO STOLE HALF OF YOUR BIKINI, I'D BE HAPPY TO COMPENSATE YOU FOR YOUR LOSS.

ME: I'M PERFECTLY CAPABLE OF BUYING MY OWN BIKINIS, THANK YOU. BUT IF YOU WERE REALLY SORRY, YOU COULD RETURN THE ONES YOU STOLE.

MR. UNDERHILL: NOT A CHANCE.

I burst out laughing.

ME: I GAVE YOU THIS NUMBER FOR EMERGENCIES ONLY. GLOATING ABOUT SWIMSUIT THEFT DOES NOT CONSTITUTE AN EMERGENCY.

MR. UNDERHILL: I MISSED YOU. DOES THAT COUNT?

I stared at the message for a long time.

He missed me?

The butterflies were back, or perhaps they'd never left.

ME: I'LL SEE YOU TOMORROW, MR. WOLFE.

MR. UNDERHILL: SEE YOU TOMORROW, CALLIE.

FORTY-FIVE MINUTES after he'd sent the last text message, he sent me another asking what my favorite color was. His eyes happened to be my favorite color, but I wasn't going to tell him that. I wrote "THE COLOR OF THE OCEAN," which was also true. We ended up messaging back and forth all day until we were saying goodnight via text at one am, but I didn't sleep.

TEN

"*A*re we gonna talk about what the fuck happened on Tuesday?" Matt was waiting for me at my suite when I got back from a quick run after my second-breakfast with Callie.

SHE SENT me a message letting me know when she would be coming up the cliff so I wouldn't have to order more than one meal. She bounced towards our table wearing my favorite accessory, her smile, after clearly having had a beach day that was *fine*. The kind of *fine* that left her grinning as she stepped off the elevator and not the kind of *fine* that furrowed her brow making me want to kiss it until it relaxed. This morning, she waited for me to pull out her seat.

We spent the next hour laughing, talking and teasing each other until she left me again. I felt my heart tug at her absence, even though I knew I'd see her again in a few hours.

"NOPE." I slid my keycard into the lock before opening the door which led to the kitchen. I'd also been avoiding him since the meeting.

"Fuck that." He followed me in. "What happened in there, man?"

"We got our asses kicked." I shrugged. "It happens." I started to undress and walked into the shower. I needed to hurry if I was going to meet Callie on time. Knowing her, if I was a minute late, she'd deduct it from my hour. I found myself smiling remembering her negotiating skills. I quickly lathered up, rinsed off, turned off the shower and wrapped a towel around my waist. Matt was sitting on my bed, and he jumped up when I exited the bathroom.

"I saved our asses in there," he yelled. Now, I had to stop. I turned to face him.

"You did?" I raised an eyebrow. "From what I remember, you lost your temper, screamed about not having a contract in writing and got your ass handed to you, in a file folder." I laughed. "How did you not see that coming?" I went back to getting ready. I pulled a white polo on over my tank top and stepped into a pair of khaki cargo shorts.

"Somebody had to say something," he shot back. *"You're so*

beautiful," he bellowed in a deep ridiculous voice. "What the hell was that? You sounded like a lunatic."

"Hey, does this shirt look wrinkled?" I smoothed the front of my shirt with one hand before I grabbed my wallet and sunglasses with the other.

"No, it's fine," he replied, before shaking his head furiously, "Wait, what? Where are you going? We have to figure out how to fix this."

"Matt." I grabbed his shoulders and gave him a small shake. "It's gonna be fine. Remember the Lasky proposition hearing?"

"Yeah, we were hung over. It was a fucking disaster. I thought we were finished."

"And yet," I spread my arms wide backing away from him grinning, "here we are." I stomped into a pair of white Pumas and headed towards the door. I smacked my forehead and jogged back into the living room where my suit jacket was still draped over an armchair. I slid the folded piece of paper out the pocket, taking care not to disturb its other contents and shoved Callie's note in my pocket. I gave Matt a two finger salute as I hustled past him. "Hang out. Have some beer. Enjoy the pool. The view from the balcony is amazing. We'll figure all this shit out later."

CALLIE ASKED me to meet her at two o'clock at a place called Oistin's in Christ Church. There was no street and no number. This didn't seem to be a problem for my driver. I showed him the paper, he nodded and sped off. I was expecting an upscale beach club, but I was greeted by what looked like a beachfront flea market. I started to think I was in the wrong place.

"This is Oistin's," I asked, "in Christs Church?"

"The one and only." I paid him and exited the car. I took a few steps towards the beach when I heard a familiar voice.

"Well, Mr. Wolfe," she called laughing. "I'm glad you could make it. I was starting to worry." I glanced down at my watch. It was 1:52.

I turned to face her. Callie's beauty caught me off guard again. Her long curls were flowing and bouncing in the breeze. She was wearing a pair of pink shorts that look like they'd been painted on underneath a black V-necked Rolling Stones tee. The red lips and protruding tongue made a sharp contrast with the tight black shirt, and I wonder if she'd worn it to taunt me. She was wearing a black pair of Tom's and tapping her left foot in mock impatience with her arms crossing her chest, pushing her breasts up and together. She was grinning a thousand-watt smile, and I couldn't believe how much I'd missed her though I had seen her a few hours ago at breakfast.

"Welcome to Oistin's," she declared.

"What is this place?"

"This," she gestured behind herself, "is where you get the best flying fish in all of the Caribbean."

I raised my eyebrows. "They serve food here?"

She had to be kidding, but on closer inspection, I did see stands with large grills topped with all kinds of delicious smelling things to eat.

"You shouldn't judge something by its appearance." She was right about that. Where was that nugget of wisdom before our meeting? I might have had a fighting chance. "C'mon, Mr. Wolfe." She slipped her hand into mine, my heart skipped a beat, and I felt a familiar tugging in my shorts as she pulled me towards a row of canopies.

"One order of flying fish, please." The wind had blown her hair into her face, and she tucked it behind her ear, "and two rum punches."

"I'll get you the rum punches, but I'm sorry, dear," the woman under the first çanopy said, "no more flying fish until tonight. We sold the last platter to that gentleman there." She pointed to a tall, thin man, a shade lighter than Callie with short curly hair, carrying two large platters of what looked like giant fish sticks to a nearby picnic table. Callie gave me a sad smile and shrugged her shoulders.

"Hold on." I started walking towards the picnic table. "Excuse me, sir…"

"What are you doing?" she hissed while tugging on my bicep.

"Excuse me, sir," I continued, as he looked up, "I'll give you a hundred dollars for one of those plates of flying fish." He stared at me in disbelief and started to bellow laughter.

"Well, Claudette fries up a mean flying fish, but I don't

know if it's that good." He was still laughing, and he was joined by a tall woman with ample hips, and a rich brown complexion that I assumed was his wife.

"What's so funny, Paul," she asked, placing a hand on his shoulder.

"This young man has offered to buy this plate of flying fish for a hundred US." He was still laughing.

"Well, then let him, you fool," she almost screamed. "I have a freezer full of flying fish at home."

"Nah, Nadine, look at him." He gestured to me. "He's trying to impress this young lady." He indicated Callie, who was still holding my bicep and almost dying of embarrassment. I was starting to feel a little self-conscious, myself.

"Yeah," Nadine replied. "I remember you doing a lot of fool things to try to get my attention; none as foolish as paying a hundred US for a plate of flying fish, but foolish enough." She gave Paul's shoulder a shove, and he smiled wrapping his arm around her waist and giving her a squeeze.

"I'm so sorry," Callie piped up. "He's never been to Barbados, and I brought him here to try the flying fish. I'm sorry we bothered you..."

"Ah, come on now, girl," he chuckled. "You're not bothering us. You should be proud to have a man that wants to make you happy and I haven't laughed like that in years." He started laughing again. Nadine looked at us, tilted her head at Paul and rolled her eyes.

"I'll tell you what," Paul continued, turning his attention to me when he caught his breath. "I will *give you* this plate of flying fish for nothing, and you can *give me* two hundred US and Nadine and I will take you and your lady on a little cruise on our boat. We had another couple book a private cruise and cancel at the last minute. You can see some flying fish in action."

I looked at Callie. She was beaming and nodding.

"Oh no," I said with mock disappointment, and she looked up me confused. "I don't know if we have enough time." I made a dramatic show of looking at my watch. "You see I only have an hour before, ow!" Callie punched me in the arm and stepped in front of me.

"Yes, sir. We would like that very much." She looked at Nadine, tilted her head at me and rolled her eyes. "We'll buy a round of drinks." She grabbed my hand and pulled me toward Claudette's kiosk. "What am I going to do with you, Alexander Wolfe?"

"Hey," I put my hands up defensively, "you already threatened to sue me for breach of contract once this week. I'm being cautious." I looked down at her smirking. "And that's for not telling me how old you were." I winked at her.

Without warning, she reached up, grabbed the back of my head and pulled me into a kiss. It was like the elevator happened ages ago and it felt incredible to kiss her again. One hand flew to her waist and the other to her fragrant curls. I squeezed her body into mine, lifting her onto her toes and holding her in place while I reacquainted myself with those soft luscious lips. We were interrupted by a loud cough. Claudette had her hands on her hips, her eyebrow raised and her lips pursed with a hint of a smile.

"Are you gonna order something or just make babies?" she said.

We cleared our throats and smiled at each other. Callie did the ordering.

"Four Banks, four shots of Mount Gay, and one rum punch." She reached into her back pocket, and I put my hand out to stop her. She pushed it away and said, "You can put your money away, Mr. Wolfe. I'm already impressed."

She placed two brightly colored bills on the counter and gave me a sexy smile and wink. I was ready to toss her over my shoulder and run all the way back to my suite at The Sterling.

Callie expertly tucked the four shots of rum between her fingers while balancing the rum punch between her palms. I grabbed the bottles of beer still not believing my luck. I let her walk in front of me so I could continue to stare. I watched the curve of her sweet round ass sway in opposition to her long mane of curls. My body was already missing the feeling of hers pressed against it. We mercifully made to the table, and I wished I wore baggier shorts.

Callie passed out the drinks, and we downed the shots with a toast to fools and flying fish. I chased it with a swig of beer.

"So are all Barbadians this friendly?" I asked.

"It's Bajans," Callie corrected me, "and yes, we are, for the most part." She smiled before adding, "But never cross a Bajan woman. They hold grudges like you wouldn't believe."

"You're not lying there, girl," shouted Paul, "this one," He jerked a thumb at Nadine, "has been mad at me about the same thing for over fifteen years." The smile on Nadine's face faded, and her eyes narrowed at Paul.

"You threw away my wedding gown," she shouted.

"By accident," he countered. An argument erupted. Callie and I looked at each other biting our lips to keep from laughing.

"Here." She offered me a bite of the infamous flying fish. "Try it."

Leaning forward, I took a bite. It was crispy, flaky and delicious. I didn't know if it was the fish itself or the look of joy on Callie's face while she watched me eat, but it might have been the best thing I've ever tasted. I watched as she bit into another piece, closing her eyes and savoring the taste.

It might have been the second best thing I've ever tasted.

ELEVEN

*A*lexander Wolfe had truly surprised me, and I couldn't remember ever smiling so much in my life. Not only was he incredibly handsome and an amazing kisser, but he was also sweet, kind, funny and even more adorably charming.

We had only met Paul and Nadine an hour ago, and they were just as enamored with Alex as I was, once they'd stopped arguing. They were already planning future fishing excursions and talking about sailing because, of course, Alex knew how to sail. My dad had tried to teach me over the years, but he gave me up as a lost cause. Who cares about knots and booms, when you can lounge on the deck soaking up the sun?

Alex was hanging on Paul's every word, but he kept a hand on my thigh giving it the occasional squeeze. I was leaning forward on his back with my arm around his waist and my chin resting on his shoulder. It just felt right, like we were made to fit together.

We learned Paul and Nadine had been married for over twenty years and hosting private cruises on their boat for just as long. Paul had moved on to talking about rum, and if Alex wasn't enjoying his crash course in all things Barbados, he didn't give a clue. He mentioned the rum punch I'd purchased.

"Well, he hasn't tried the rum punch in Barbados before." I gave Paul and Nadine a knowing smirk.

"I've had rum punch before," he answered defensively before he grabbed the plastic cup, whipped the straw out, brought the cup to his nose and took a cautious whiff. He jerked his head back slightly, furrowing his brow and exhaling.

"Are you gonna sit there smelling all day or drink it, man?" Paul laughed.

Alex looked at me and raised an eyebrow. I raised mine in response as if to say *well, are you?* He smiled and tossed his head back downing half the cup in one gulp. His face screwed up, and he let out a loud *ah* sound.

"That's good," he said almost as if he couldn't believe it. Then, he added, "but it burns." He lightly pounded his chest with his fist, "and it's spicy." He grabbed the cup and downed the rest of the punch in another gulp causing the table to erupt in laughter. "What's in this?"

"It's in the name, man," Paul chuckled, "rum and," he held up a fist dramatically, "PUNCH!"

Paul, Alex and I laughed. Nadine just smiled and shook

her head. I got the feeling this wasn't the first time Paul told his rum punch joke.

———

THEIR BOAT WAS A BIG, beautiful luxury catamaran. There was a broad blue stripe on the side with the word, NADINE painted in big block letters underneath. I was secretly relieved because catamarans were my favorite type of boat. I loved them all: glass bottom boats, small sailboats, even submarines, but catamarans reminded me of little floating islands, and Paul and Nadine's had an upper deck with a seating and dining area and lower deck with another seating area, full bathrooms, a kitchen, and bedrooms.

Alex grabbed my waist and lifted me onto the steps before climbing on himself. Once on deck, he gave me a kiss, and a patted my ass.

"Go grab me a seat before all the good ones are taken," he joked with a wink, and I headed towards the deck chairs. I settled into one, and I saw Alex and Paul talking. They were too far away to hear, and I couldn't read lips, but I saw Alex making a circular gesture with his finger and then Paul held up five fingers. Alex removed six bills from the wallet he'd pulled from the pocket of his shorts. Paul laughed and tried to return one of the bills. Alex whispered something into his ear and clapped him on the shoulder. Paul laughed and nodded accepting the extra bill. Alex jogged over to me grinning.

"What was that about?" I asked as he slid into the chair beside me before pulling me onto his lap.

"Nothing," he kissed my forehead as I snuggled into his chest, "guy stuff."

"What are you up to, Mr. Wolfe?" I jerked my head up and narrowed my eyes at him. He kissed me.

"I could ask you the same question, Ms. Sterling," he said before kissing me again. I loved the way his lips felt.

"I don't know what you're talking about?"

"I'm talking about that rum punch." He raised his eyebrows looking scandalized, and I laughed remembering his face after the first gulp. "I think you're trying to get me drunk so you could have your way with me."

"Would that be a problem?" I twisted my body and straddled him giving him full access to my lips. He shook his head in response and placed both of his hands on my hips, and I could feel his erection pressing between my legs again. This time I was rocking my hips back and forth feeling its length slide up and down my sensitive folds. Our kiss deepened, and I felt his tongue part my lips and begin to explore my mouth. My breath got heavy as the warm waves of pleasure washed over me. Then I felt the hum of the boat's engine and felt a lurch as we pulled away from the dock. I broke our kiss.

"Hey," I called to him breathlessly. "We have to stop."

"No," he whispered, "we don't." He tried to kiss me again.

"We're on the deck of a boat." He was nibbling my neck, and I started to giggle.

"Yeah, I know," he whispered again, "and I don't care."

"Well, I do," I laughed, and motioned to Paul and Nadine. "I don't want to be rude."

"Fine," he said, putting on the pouty face of a boy who had just been told he had to wait until the end of his birthday party to open presents. Then he smiled at me.

I got up and walked towards Nadine feeling Alex's eyes on me as I walked away from him. She was headed towards us with a tray carrying two glasses of champagne, and a plate of fruit and cheese.

"Thank you, I can carry this." I reached for the tray but she expertly tugged it out my reach, smiling. "You don't have to go to all of this trouble for us."

"Oh." she smiled. "It's no trouble. To tell the truth, we're lucky you came along after that other couple canceled. We had everything prepared anyway; the linens washed, the beds made, the refrigerator stocked. " I started looking around.

"Go downstairs and have a look. It's yours for the whole day. Call if you need anything. Paul and I will be up here if you need us."

"The whole day?" I asked in shock. She smiled.

"Your boyfriend didn't tell you?"

"No," I smiled shaking my head, Alex was talking to Paul again. They must have been discussing the catamaran because Alex had somehow convinced Paul to let him steer. He was gripping the wheel with one hand and gesturing to different parts of the boat with the other. "My *boyfriend* didn't tell me."

I descended the staircase into the lower deck of the boat.

The layout was magnificent. I knew the boat was big but seeing the lower deck made me instantly think of the magic tent from the *Harry Potter* series. The abundance of windows added to the illusion, and if it weren't for the rhythmic rocking, I would have forgotten I was on a boat. I was standing in a large sitting room lined with white plush couches. I took a step towards the front of the ship to see the rest of the layout when I heard footsteps on the stairs behind me.

I turned to see Alex's form darken the stairwell. He jumped the rest of the flight of stairs and landed in front of me.

"Hi." He grinned down at me.

"Hi." I smiled up at him.

He scooped me under the thighs and lifted me onto his waist. I wrapped my legs around his massive torso, my arms around his neck and began kissing him like a woman possessed. He returned my kiss and started stomping through the deck until he found the door to the bedroom. He pushed it open and tossed me on the bed.

"I've been waiting for this all week." He gave me a hungry smile and lowered himself to the bed. He kissed my lips softly and stood again, taking one of my legs, caressing it gently with his fingertips from my thigh to ankle and removed my shoe. He grabbed the other leg and did the same.

He unbuttoned my shorts and slid them down my legs before tossing them over his shoulder. He hooked his fingertips into the elastic of my panties and pulled them down as he knelt at the foot of the bed. He began to trail kisses up my legs as he slowly pushed my knees apart. Each kiss was sending little jolts of electricity through my body, and the anticipation was intense as he got closer and closer.

After what seemed like an eternity, he planted a kiss on my outer lips, and I could feel his tongue parting me and exploring my wetness. I began to moan.

"God, I fucking love the way you taste." He peppered my inner thighs with kisses, licks, and gentle nibbles before swirling his tongue through my sensitive folds.

"I love the way you taste me," I sighed, running my fingers through his dark hair.

There was a rush of cool air as he pulled away from me, and in an instant, we were face to face on the bed.

"What are you doing?" I whispered breathlessly. "Why did you stop?" I was almost pleading.

"Because," He reached out, pushed my hair out of my face and tucked it behind my ear, "I want to see your beautiful face when you come for me. I missed it the first time." He planted a kiss on my lips, and I could taste myself on his tongue. One of his hands reached down my stomach over my t-shirt and in-between my thighs. He slipped the tip of his two middle fingers into my entrance and used the lubrication to slide over my clitoris making me twitch and jerk with pleasure. The thick fingers pushed back and forth with Alex's eyes fixed on mine. He was smiling at me, and I smiled back. He began to make circular motions with his fingers and picked up speed. My mouth opened, and my eyes widened as I felt the climax build. Alex's smile faded, and his look intensified as he focused on bringing me closer to an explosion.

"Yes, beautiful," he whispered, "let go."

I did as I was told and it felt good ceding control to this man. I arched my back and squeezed my eyes shut as my body rocked from the climax. My thighs involuntarily clamped onto Alex's hand but did nothing to slow his movements. My moaning intensified, and I felt Alex's mouth closed over mine, kissing me until my orgasm faded.

I flopped back onto the bed trying to catch my breath. Alex was admiring the shiny evidence of my arousal on the tips of his fingers before he put them in his mouth and pulled them out slowly, giving me a dirty grin. The muscles between my thighs clenched in an aftershock.

"Callie," he said, very matter of factly, still sporting that sexy grin, "I *need* to be inside you."

I tried to stifle a giggle.

"So, do you have any other appointments...?"

I shook my head.

"…any other surprises or secrets I should know about?"

I did have one, but wasn't something that he should know about, so I shook my head again smiling.

"Is your name really Callie?"

"It's Calypso, actually," I said with a smile. His eyes widened.

"Calypso, like the music?" he asked.

"No," I started clawing at his shorts, "Calypso like the goddess." I kissed him. "No more questions, Mr. Wolfe."

TWELVE

CALYPSO

*H*e pulled me on top of him and lifted my shirt over my head tossing it onto the floor. He grabbed the two handfuls of my breasts and brought them to his face, kissing, nibbling and sucking them before yanking the straps of my bra down freeing them. He reached for the clasp. After a few seconds of his swearing and fumbling fingers, I pulled my arms out of the straps, reached behind my back and unsnapped my bra causing it to fall away.

"Thank you," he whispered against my lips with a smile. His hands were roaming my fully naked torso.

"You're welcome," I answered. "Now it's your turn." I reached down and tugged at the hem of his polo shirt. He pulled it over his head, and it joined the growing pile of clothes on the floor with his tank top close behind.

We were kissing furiously again, and he began pushing himself out of his shorts. I broke our kiss, slid down to stand at the foot of the bed and help him, tugging off his shorts and boxer briefs. His cock bursts forth unencumbered and full.

Feeling his dick rub against me through his shorts did not to prepare me how big it really was. I was the biggest one I'd ever seen up close. Not that I'd seen that many.

The thought of Alex filling me up both excited me and made me a little nervous but I was never a woman to back away from a challenge. I tucked my bottom lip between my teeth and leaned forward to wrap my hand around his fullness. Alex shuddered as my grip closed around his girth. The tips of my middle finger and thumb barely grazed each other. His hand clasped my shoulder when I leaned forward licking my lips.

"What are you doing?" His voice was a rough whisper, and his chest was heaving.

"What do you think?" I shot him a sexy grin and stroked his length causing him to shudder again.

"Callie," he panted, "and I can't believe I'm saying this, but if your lips come any closer to my dick right now, I'm going to fucking lose it. The first time I come with you I want your sweet pussy wrapped around me while you're screaming my name with your ankles on my shoulder." He carefully removed my hand from his cock, and I could see a tiny drop of pre-cum glistening on his thick crown. His filthy words galvanized me. I reached out and swiped the slick bead of liquid with my index finger and tucked it between my lips.

"I *am* very flexible." I grinned again after I removed the

finger from my mouth.

"Fuck me," he whispered, but I was sure he hadn't meant to speak.

"If you insist, Mr. Wolfe." I slid the condom Alex retrieved from his shorts out of his hand and crawled on top of him.

"Are you sure you don't me to…" I swiped my tongue over my bottom lip and raised an eyebrow.

"Jesus fucking Christ," he groaned. His aching need was etched on his pained expression and his impossibly hard cock that had begun leaking again. "You're trying to kill me, aren't you? This was the plan all along, wasn't it?"

I giggled. "You figured me out. So, if the game is up, I guess I should go…" I tried to rise, hoping I wouldn't get far. I didn't before Alex's hands shot out bracketing my waist holding me in place.

"I could think of worse ways to go," he whispered. I leaned forward and brushed my lips over his. "Callie, please. The condom."

"Well, since you asked so nicely." I tore open the foil package and carefully rolled it on as he twitched and jerked in my grasp. The instant I got the condom on, Alex sat up still clutching my hips and flipped me onto my back.

I took a deep breath and braced myself, suddenly apprehensive. My body tensed and Alex sensed it. He leaned down, planted the softest kiss on my lips and ran the pad of his index finger down the bridge of my nose.

I drew in a deep breath and smiled at Alex hoping he couldn't read my expression. He didn't seem convinced.

"Callie," His expression was serious and tinged with concern, "Are you a virgin?"

"No, but it's been a while…" *A while* was an understatement, but I would keep that to myself. "…and you have a very big —"

He cut me off mid-sentence, and I could see the ghost of a smile haunting his gorgeous face.

"Please." He kissed me. "If you finish that sentence I'm gonna need another condom. Don't worry, Goddess," He kissed me again, "I'll be gentle."

He slid a hand between us, grazing my sex and making me shiver before gliding his fingertips down my thigh where he found the back of my knee urging my legs further apart. I hooked the other leg around his waist and pressed my heel into the firm muscles of his ass, eliciting a deep guttural grunt that seemed to come from somewhere deep inside of him. He lowered himself, propping his torso up on his elbows and kissing me once more. Those blue eyes were gazing at me again with the same supplicating expression from the elevator, eyebrows raised with a plea so palpable, no words were needed. I smiled and nodded, reaching up and entangling my fingers in his hair. The feelings that followed; him pushing himself into me, stretching me was an exquisite mixture of pain and pleasure. He was taking his time, nudging himself into my core inch by scintillating inch, rocking his hips back forth, pressing in further with each return.

"Oh. My. God!" he breathed into my neck. I answered his exclamation with a loud moan of ecstasy that I hadn't planned and couldn't control. It had been a long time, but I never remembered sex being like this. The sensations were delicious and overwhelming. He stopped and leaned up, gazing at me.

"Are you okay?" he asked with his sapphire eyes full of concern.

How could anything not be okay with this man? I nodded and kissed him again.

"Do you trust me, Callie?"

It was such an odd question to ask during sex, but my answer was complicated. We wouldn't be in this bed if I didn't trust him, but I was still keeping secrets from him, and I suppose he had his own secrets. But in this moment, nothing else existed, but the two of us and nothing else mattered. For as long as we were wrapped in each other's arms in this room, I trusted him completely.

I nodded again. "Yes, I trust you," I whispered. He sealed his lips over mine, and I felt his body flex as he gave me all of himself. He started to move in and out of me again: rhythmically, slowly and beautifully. The pain dissolved, and I relaxed as pleasure took over.

My lover's face was buried in my neck, and I could feel his warm, gentle breathing with every thrust. He grazed my clitoris every time our hips met intensifying my arousal.

Alex began to pick up speed. He reached behind himself and pressed one of my thighs into his hip, digging his fingers into the flesh. I responded by hooking my ankles together and squeezing my legs around his waist. He was murmuring sweet everythings to me while planting tiny kisses behind my ear.

My orgasm was close, and I wanted Alex's mouth on me again. I grabbed the sides of his face and crushed our lips together. Our tongues intertwined, and Alex's thrusts intensified. He reached behind his back again, found my knee and slid his hand down my lower leg to my ankle and placed it on his shoulder. The ease at which my body bent to his will surprised him.

"Fuck me," he whispered to himself again. The new position made the sensitive gathering of nerves that Alex had been priming more accessible, and I gasped preparing to tumble off a cliff of ecstasy, head first into a mind-blowing, body rocking climax.

My entire body tensed and I screamed his name as he predicted.

Alex's orgasm was right behind mine. "Fuck, Callie, Fuck!" he bellowed. He clenched and relaxed a few times before lowering himself onto me and kissing me again.

"That's it," he gasped, his chest rapidly rising and falling. "I'm dead. You killed me, and this is heaven."

I managed a weak chuckle with the last iota of strength my body possessed. He slid himself out of me and flopped next to me on the bed, catching his breath.

"God, I'm crazy about you, Calypso." He kissed my shoulder and climbed out of bed, returning with a warm damp cloth. He cleaned me before climbing in beside me, wrapping his arm around my waist and pulling me close to him.

I laid blinking for a minute, trying to process what I thought I'd heard him say. It was unmistakable, but I couldn't have heard him correctly.

"Alex?" I whispered finally.

"Hmm," he replied lazily, "so I'm not Mr. Wolfe anymore." He playfully bit my shoulder.

"Did you say," I hesitated, wanting to make sure I hadn't gone completely insane, "that you were *crazy* about me?"

"Yup." He kissed my shoulder.

"Did you mean it?"

"I did." He used his elbow to prop his head up on his fist, and he faced me. "I thought I was *crazy* about you in the elevator and after the meeting, I knew I'd be *crazy* ever to let you go again but now…" He squeezed his arm around my waist, pulling me closer. "I've never felt this way before about anyone and I really want to see where this goes." He planted two more kisses on my shoulder.

I was laughing. It was a giddy sort of laughter, like the kind I got from the gas at the dentist. It must have been all of the endorphins.

I couldn't actually be this happy, could I?

"And I'm not entirely sure, because you are an enigma, wrapped in a mystery, tied up in a riddle but," He kissed my nose, "I'm pretty sure you feel the same way about me." He looked at me raising an eyebrow.

"I do." The words tumbled out of my mouth before I could think about it and I grabbed the sides of his face, kissing him again.

"Finally," he shouted into the otherwise empty bedroom. "We agree on something."

I laughed, and he pulled me on top of him, growling and tickling me. He stopped and took my chin and turned my face towards his.

"Listen." He was serious again. "I still don't understand what's so important about The Sterling—"

I opened my mouth to protest.

"—but—"

I narrowed my eyes.

"—but, it's important to you, and you're important to me. So, I'm gonna tell Matt to back off."

"Do you mean it?" Tears stung my eyes, and I tried to blink them away.

"Yes. If I say it, I mean it, especially to you." He used his thumb to wipe away a tear and kissed me. "Plus, I see what happens when you cross a Bajan woman." He pointed upward. "I don't want you yelling at me for fifteen years."

I laughed, and he pulled me into a kiss. I snuggled into the crook of his arm and closed my eyes.

THIRTEEN

ALEXANDER

Callie's small, warm body was pressed against mine. Her eyes were closed, and she was breathing deeply, sound asleep. As I watched her, I realized that I'd never seen her like this. The Callie Sterling I tried so desperately to spend every minute with for the last few days was constantly on guard and carrying the weight of the world on her shoulders. In my arms, her face was angelic, calm and she was at peace. There was even the faint curve of a smile on her lips. I had given her that. In return, she had given me her trust and more happiness in the last three days than I could remember in...more happiness than I could ever remember. Every professional victory felt amazing, but it was nothing compared to the unconditional bliss wrapped in every single one of Callie's smiles.

I looked out the window and saw that the sun would be setting soon. I pressed my lips to her forehead, and she stirred.

"Hi." She looked up at me and blinked before a smile lit up her entire face.

"Hi," I whispered, before pressing my lips to hers. "The sun is setting soon. Do you want to go swimming, then have dinner?"

"On the boat?" she asked. I nodded, squeezing her into me.

"I don't have a swimsuit."

"Paul said there were some in the closet."

"I'm not wearing a used bathing suit." She scrunched up her face, and I couldn't stop myself from planting a kiss on her nose.

"They're all new. Go check it out."

She narrowed her eyes at me and climbed out of bed. Her body was gorgeous as I watched her stand at the foot of the bed with her back to me, stretching and pulling her long hair into a bun and fastening it with a tie. My eyes roved over the swell of her breasts, the dip of her small waist and to the curve of her round ass. There was a smattering of sexy dimples on her thighs that I wanted to explore with my tongue. Maybe, we'd have to skip dinner after all.

She walked to the closet and began pulling out swimsuits, before turning to me with a skeptical expression.

"Did you plan this?" Her eyes narrowed, and I could see her laying the foundation to rebuild the wall I'd spent the better part of a week dismantling.

I jumped out of bed and stepped behind her wrapping my arms around her waist and kissing her shoulder.

"No. I didn't plan this. *I mean it.* See," I pointed to the fully stocked closet, "there are all different sizes." I could tell she wasn't convinced. "Look at this." I pulled out the largest pair of men's swim trunks and pushed my arm through one of the leg holes. It was a perfect fit. Callie burst out laughing. "Don't you think I would have made sure Paul and Nadine had my size?"

"Fine." She was still grinning as she turned to face me. She ran her fingertips over my three days of stubble. "But what are you going to swim in?"

"I'm good in my boxers," I leaned forward to kiss her. "That is if you can keep your hands to yourself."

"I'll do my best, Mr. Wolfe." She stood on tip-toe and wrapped her arms around my neck. I leaned forward. "But I can't make any promises." Our lips met, and my hands got busy exploring the contours of her body. She pulled our faces apart. "Please tell me you have another condom."

I grinned and kissed her again before scooping her under her knees and carrying her back the bed.

———

WE ONLY HAD a few minutes left of daylight to swim. I'd been swimming since I was a kid and I thought I was pretty good, but Callie moved through the ocean like she was born for the water. My sexy little goddess was a jock, a nerd, a joker and also a mermaid.

We swam back to the boat and sat on the steps with Callie tucked between my legs as we dangled our toes in The Atlantic to watch the sun set.

I wrapped my arms around her waist and grazed my nose across her shoulder savoring the way the smell of the ocean mingled with her already intoxicating scent. Callie scanned the glittering water as if she were searching for something. Then she squeezed my arm with one hand and pointed with the other.

"Holy shit," I whispered. "Are those…"

"Mmm hmm." She nodded and grinned.

About a dozen or so thin silvery blue fish were taking turns leaping out of the sea, spreading what looked like long sparkling wings and gliding a few feet out of the water before diving back beneath the waves. We were silent as the school of flying fish continued to jump and splash past the NADINE. I watched the aquatic show in awe, as Callie watched me. I couldn't stop thinking that every experience seemed enchanting because I was with her.

"They're amazing," I whispered.

"And delicious," she added, making me laugh again. I tightened my arms around her waist.

NADINE BROUGHT our dinner to a small table on the deck of the boat. It was flying fish but sautéed with rice and vegetables served with glasses of Chardonnay. We asked her and Paul to join us but they politely refused.

Callie and I ate in mostly silence. I suspected it was due to our full afternoon of sex and swimming. Dessert was rum cake and ice cream.

"Alex, what is that?" Callie pointed over my shoulder. I swiveled in my chair to look but didn't see anything. Shrugging, I turned back to question her just in time to see her tucking her fork into her mouth and wearing a mischievous smile, her cheeks stuffed like a chipmunk. There was a large piece of rum cake missing from my plate. The laugh that erupted from my chest totally took me by surprise. This woman possessed some kind of magic over me that I couldn't understand, but I never wanted to end.

"You know, you could've asked." I grinned.

"That's no fun," she said before reaching across the table and breaking off another piece of my cake with her fork. She was right. Her way was a lot more fun.

"What's wrong with your cake?" I asked, unable to take my eyes off of her.

"I don't know," she replied in mock confusion, "yours just tastes better for some reason." She speared the piece with her fork and held it out to me. "See?"

I leaned forward, closed my mouth around the tines of the

fork and leaned back. She was right again. Rum cake had become my new favorite cake. She grinned at me.

"Come home with me." I blurted it out so quickly that I couldn't remember if I had phrased it as a question. Her face registered genuine confusion this time, and she blinked.

"To New York?"

Shit. I meant to my suite at The Sterling. What did it mean that I had referred to my place in Barbados as *home*? It was a slip. It didn't mean anything.

Did it?

And what about New York? I should've been back in the city two days ago, but I extended my stay at The Sterling for a month. At the time, I told myself it was for work, but I didn't even believe that. Matt was the most competent person at my company and the only department head I never worried about. If I dropped off of the face of the earth tomorrow Matt would be the only person who could— I stopped myself mid-thought.

What the fuck was I thinking?

"I meant my suite."

"Oh." She bit her lip in contemplation. I wondered if she was thinking the same things I was.

What would she say if I did ask her to come to New York with me?

"I should probably go home. Dad would be worried."

I nodded trying to mask my disappointment at the prospect of spending a night without Callie at arm's reach.

"Hey," I looked around, seeing no sign of Paul or Nadine. "How long has it been since you..." I trailed off and waggled my eyebrows.

"Since I've been interrogated by the world's nosiest man?" She raised her eyebrows, and I laughed again. "Not very long."

"The world's nosiest man with a very big..." I trailed off raising an eyebrow.

"Ego?" she replied without missing a beat, making me smile. Damn, I was falling harder for her every second.

"Okay, fine. You don't have to tell me."

She reached for another piece of my cake, and I tugged it out of her reach. She tilted her head and narrowed her eyes.

"Extortion, Mr. Underhill? Why am I not surprised?" She was joking but didn't know how true her words were. Hopefully, that was a topic for a day that would never come. "Why do you want to know anyway? Was it bad?" Her eyes flicked away before meeting mine again.

"What? No," I said quickly. "It was amazing." I saw her relax slightly. "It was..." I was suddenly at a loss for words the back of my neck was getting hot for some reason. It was the best sex of my life. Words couldn't describe it. "Hey, I'm asking the questions here, Ms. Sterling."

The corners of her mouth quirked in amusement. She narrowed her eyes, and I could tell she was sizing me up, debating whether or not she should answer.

Finally, she said, "Five years." Her eyes flicked away and back to mine, waiting for a reaction.

Five years? How? Not that I'm complaining, but how?

She chuckled at my shocked expression. "Does that surprise you?"

"A little," I lied. "You're so…"

"Black?" She smirked.

"You're never going let me forget that are you?"

"Let you forget the first time you told me I was beautiful, while we were in a conference room in front of six lawyers, the head of your real estate division, my father and a stenographer? *Not a chance.*" She winked at me before her eyes went wide and she gasped. "I should request a copy of the transcript." She was biting her lip trying to keep her laughter under control. I narrowed my eyes shaking my head at her.

"There weren't six lawyers in that room."

"Yes, there were." She grinned again. "Two of them were first-year associates and not assigned to The Sterling, but," She shrugged, "still lawyers."

"I knew it."

Her laughter died down and gave me an adorable look of mock pity evidently feeling like she'd tortured me enough. There were worse forms of torture, like the one I'd be facing later that night in the empty king sized bed in my suite.

"Well, growing up on a tiny island at a place like The Sterling can feel like living in a fishbowl. Imagine growing up with dozens of 'aunts, uncles and cousins' watching your every move and reporting back to your parents. I had my first serious boyfriend when I was sixteen. He was a little too vocal about our relationship. It got back to some of the guys in the kitchen and," she paused, "let's just say they sorted him out and we broke up soon after that. He might have deserved it, but you can imagine... Word spread quickly, and there weren't a lot of boys lining up to date me after that. They weren't exactly lining up before." She shrugged.

"Freshman year, I thought things would be different. It was a fresh start in a big city where no one knew me. I dated a few guys, but they never lasted long. They either treated me like an idiot: despite being able to hold my own at one of the most prestigious schools in the world, a secret: fun to spend time with, but not someone you'd introduce to your family or friends or worst of all, a fetish: I mean, if I was called an '*exotic beauty*,'" She rolled her eyes and sketched air quotes, " had my accent mocked or asked about my eye color by one more asshole looking to get me into bed, I'd turn homicidal.

"I dated a guy for a couple of weeks who was obsessed with my eyes. They were all he could talk about. Finally, one day I'd had enough and drew him a Punnett square and explained that my mother can trace our ancestry through both the Irish indentured servants and the African slaves of Barbados. I suddenly became less interesting when my '*exotic*' appearance is less magical and more due to secondary school science combined with a history of human cruelty," she said and shook her head with a tiny half smirk. "Apparently, slavery is a real…what did he say?" She made a dramatic thinking face, looking off to her side, "…ah, yes… '*boner killer*.'" She huffed out a mirthless chuckle.

Her face grew serious, and she picked at her cake with her fork. "Wharton is stressful enough, so it was better to just focus on my studies without…distractions." She sighed and looked at me apprehensively.

"I'm…sorry." I didn't know what else to say. I made a mental note to never use the word *exotic* again to describe anything. I briefly contemplated asking for the names of every little prick she dated at Wharton, starting with *Mr. Boner Killer*, and making sure they never rose above the ranks of a mail clerk, but instead, I reached for her hand and squeezed. Her lips quirked into a smile.

"Are you though?" She returned my squeeze, and I was relieved to see her relax again.

"Not entirely, because maybe you wouldn't be sitting here with me." I leaned forward and took her other hand. Her smile widened.

"I think I earned that cake, Alex."

"A deal is a deal."

FOURTEEN

ALEXANDER

*W*e showered and made love a final time. I held Callie in my arms until Nadine knocked on the bedroom door announcing we would be docking in fifteen minutes. I would've paid Paul to sail us to Australia if it meant never having to let go of my goddess, but I was pretty sure kidnapping wasn't the way to end the greatest day of my life.

I INSISTED on walking Callie to her house, anything to spend another second with her. The Closer was sitting on the patio and stood when we approached.

"Dad!" Callie tensed beside me and loosened her grip on my hand briefly before she took a deep breath and squeezed it again. The small gesture made my chest swell. "You remember Alexander Wolfe."

His eyes narrowed and his lips pressed into a thin line.

His eyes darted between Callie and me and his nostrils flared slightly. Callie squeezed my hand again before releasing it, walking up to her father and kissing him on the cheek.

"Yes, I remember." His expression didn't change. I stepped forward and extended my hand. He grasped it and squeezed. Barnabas Sterling had to be well into his sixties, but his grip was firm, really fucking firm. "Bug, go in the house. I want to have a word with *Mr. Underhill.*"

Shit...Shit. Shit. Shit.

"Dad—" Callie began.

"Calypso." He cut her off.

She looked between her father and me.

"I'll be fine." I smiled at her. She kissed me on the cheek and took a step towards the house.

"This is happening, Dad. Be nice to him." She put a hand on her father's chest, and his expression softened. He smiled at her. We watched her disappear into the house. The door clicked shut and we turned to face each other.

"What the hell are you playing at, Son?" He let go of my hand, and his expression hardened. I didn't realize how tight he was squeezing until he let go and I felt the blood rushing back to my fingertips. My bicep ached from the effort of matching his grip. I focused on keeping calm. Showing weakness to The Closer wasn't an option, and the stakes were a lot higher than a resort.

"I'm not sure what you mean. I've already told Callie that we're not pursuing The Sterling."

He eyed me for a moment. His face split in a grin before he dissolved into laughter.

"Even if I believed that bullshit, this has nothing to do with The Sterling and everything to do with my daughter." He pointed to the door Callie disappeared through. "She isn't like us. She's got my brains and my eyes, but everything else is her mother's including her tender heart. She has no idea what our world is really like or what kind of people we really are."

I understood what he was saying. He was wrong about me, but why would he believe me? I wouldn't if I were him. He was right, we were all a bunch of liars and manipulators with five hundred dollar haircuts in ten thousand dollar suits. We didn't trust anyone, and no one could trust us. Except for Callie. She trusted us. That woman was intelligent, clever and shrewd, but she was also sweet and kind. Sterling was right, she wasn't like me, and that's why I needed her so much.

"Sir, I care about Callie."

He seemed to ignore my last statement. "You know, I knew your grandfather before he retired. I was sorry to hear about his passing."

I nodded solemnly.

"He was a tough old bastard, but I respected him. Based on what I've read about Wolfe Industries since you took over, it seems the apple doesn't fall far from the tree."

"Thank you."

"That wasn't a compliment. Not when it comes to someone thinking about dating my daughter."

"Sir, I don't want to be your enemy."

"You're goddamned right about that. I've been in this game a lot longer than you have. You may have my daughter fooled. Shit, you may even have yourself fooled, but I know who and what you are."

"I would never hurt Callie." I was starting to lose my temper.

"Yes. You will. Whether you intend to or not remains to be seen. So, do her a favor. Go back to New York. Go back to the boardroom. Let her find someone else who can give her the life she deserves." He could insult me. He could even insult my grandfather. I didn't give a fuck about that. But he was asking me to leave Callie, and that wasn't an option. The thought of her wrapped in someone else's arms, smiling at someone else the way she smiled at me made my chest tighten.

"I can't do that and Callie is her own woman. She should decide what she wants."

The Closer laughed again. "My daughter has decided all right. When she wants something, she goes after it. Once she makes up her mind, there's no changing it. I'll simply have to be patient and hope she realizes what you are before it's too late."

His expression hardened, and he took a step closer. "If you do hurt her, I'll be there to pick up the pieces and put them back together. And when I'm done, I will fucking bury you. Yours won't be the first body I've had to hide. I've given up everything for love once. I wouldn't hesitate to do it again."

I WAS LAYING on my bed thinking about what The Closer said. There was a reason the guy was a legend. He completely fucked me up with one sentence.

"Shit, you may even have yourself fooled, but I know who and what you are."

Was I fooling myself to think I deserved to be with someone like Callie? Her face during her confession at dinner haunted me. She pretended to be strong and unaffected, but there was real pain underneath her facade. I'd also be ready to bury the body of someone who made her feel that way, but what if that someone was me? Maybe, I should let her go before things go too far. I picked up my phone to call her when I heard the knock.

She was standing on the other side of my door looking so beautiful I couldn't speak. Her bottom lip was tucked between her teeth in an attempt to stifle the grin that lit up her face despite her attempts to hide it. Every thought of leaving her vanished making me wonder why the fuck I would have ever considered an idea so insane.

"Hi," she whispered and looked up at me.

"Hi?" I answered, and it felt like a question. "Did you sneak out?"

She laughed in response.

"I'm a grown woman. I don't sneak anywhere." She raised an eyebrow, and my dick jumped to attention.

Fuck me.

Her shoulders did a little shake when she let out a chuckle, looking into my suite then back at me. "May I come in?"

"What?" I shook my head to regain focus. "Fuck, yeah. Yes."

"If this is a bad time, I can—" She jerked a thumb over her shoulder before turning to leave, and I reached out scooped her into my arms, carrying her squealing and laughing into my suite.

Our suite.

"Alex?" I whispered to no response. Warmth radiated off his large body carrying waves of his delicious scent, traces of soap and cologne mingled with something I couldn't describe but was distinctly him. His arm was curled around my waist, and one of my lower legs was tucked between his calves. My scalp was being massaged as he took deep contented breaths in his sleep. I'd never slept with someone like this before. This felt more intimate than the night full of sex. I've shared a bed with a man before but not a man like Alex.

He carried me into his suite last night. Then we made love like it was our first time and our last time. Alex held me in his arms and we talked until we drifted off to sleep. He was so loving, attentive and interested in everything I had to say. I felt the same way about him. The notorious Alexander Wolfe who was supposed to be a ruthless corporate tyrant was someone I'd never met. Instead, I was entwined with a man who valued my intelligence, made me laugh and made me feel safe: a man I could trust.

After carefully disentangling myself from him, I gathered my clothes and tip-toed into the bathroom. The sun hadn't risen, and I was sure if I left soon, I could skip any awkward run-ins with members of the staff. Dad would definitely be awake. There was no avoiding that.

There were no spare toothbrushes, so I made do with mouthwash, splashed my face with water, pulled my hair into a ponytail, got dressed and slipped back into the bedroom, intent on making a swift getaway, planning to text him on the way to the beach.

"Hey," Alex said in a sleepy grumble while running his arm back and forth across the empty bed beside him. "Where are you going?"

"Home," I whispered. I was careful to stay out of arms reach because now that he was awake, all I wanted to do was crawl back into his arms. The look he was giving me said he wanted the same thing. "I have to change and get to the beach."

"Go to the beach from here." His outstretched arm was creeping towards me, and he was wearing the same pouty expression from the boat. I took another step back. If he touched me it, would be over.

"I don't have my bathing suit or a change of clothes. I don't even have a toothbrush."

"If you're trying to get your bikini bottoms back, forget it.

But I will order a bathing suit from the concierge, and you can use my toothbrush."

"Ugh. I'm not using your toothbrush."

"Callie," He sat up. "After the things I saw you put in your mouth last night, my toothbrush shouldn't be an issue."

My eyes went wide, I gasped and stepped forward to grab a pillow off of the bed to hit him with it. Alex seized the opportunity to grab my wrist and tugged me onto the mattress, wrapping his arms around my waist and curling his body around me.

"That's different." I used the arm that wasn't pinned underneath me to slap his thigh. He chuckled softly.

"Stay," he whispered, brushing the shell of my ear with his lips.

"I can't." I closed my eyes and succumbed to the full body tingling that the tiny kisses Alex was planting along the back of my ear were causing. "But you'll see me later today…if you want." I wasn't sure why I added the last part.

Alex wasn't either. "Of course, I want to see you later, but for now let me give you a proper goodbye." He slid a hand under my shirt and cupped it over a lace covered breast. His lips traced a trail of heat down my neck and across my chin until he found my lips. I turned my body to face him.

"Take off your clothes, Goddess," he whispered.

I did as I was told.

"GOOD MORNING." Dad greeted me with an almost bored, clipped tone that I could see right through.

"Good morning, Dad." I didn't want to hug him because I was wearing Alex's scent like a second skin and I wasn't ready to wash it off yet. "Do you want to talk about this?"

"I believe we did all the talking we're going to do last night, young lady. You're an adult, as you reminded me, perfectly capable of making your own decisions." He shook the paper he was holding for effect as if I believed for one moment he was actually reading it instead of waiting for me to come home. "Off to the beach?"

"Yeah."

"Well, have a good time, Calypso." He turned his attention to his coffee and paper.

He didn't call me Bug, once.

Yes, I was an adult, but I was still his daughter. I marched over to the table.

"Hey," I said. He looked up to face me. His expression was sad and worried tinged with annoyance. "I'm not doing this to upset you. It's not something I planned, but I really care about Alex, and he cares about me. You have your doubts about him, and I understand all of them, believe me, but please give him a chance and don't shut me out. You taught me to be independent and to trust my instincts. Well, that's what I'm doing. This is scary, but I'm happy, and I need my dad."

"Oh, Bug," he sighed. I felt my shoulders sag in relief. "You will always have me, and I trust you, but I don't trust Alexander Wolfe. I would burn this entire resort to the ground if it meant sparing you an ounce of pain, but I can't do that. It's one of the toughest things about being your father, and I'm afraid I'll never get used to it." He managed a small smile.

"I love you, Dad." I pressed a kiss to his temple.

"I love you too, Bug." He turned away from me and opened the paper again. "Well, go on. Don't keep her waiting."

TIANNA WAS LEAVING the cottage as I got to the stone path. Her smile flooded me with relief, and she flashed me an "okay" symbol, curling her thumb and finger into an "o" with her remaining three fingers extended.

"I have to run up the cliff to take care of some things, but I'll be back in about two hours. Okay, baby girl?" She kissed me on the cheek and scurried down the beach towards the elevator.

"Beautiful Barbados" by The Merrymen was playing when I stepped into the house. She looked up when she saw me and her face spread in a grin before she sauntered over to me swaying her hips. She stopped a few feet in front of me, tilted her head and narrowed her eyes.

"You look different," she said. My fingers instinctively moved to my lips where I could still feel the ghost of the body melting kiss Alex had been waiting by the elevator to give me on the way to the beach.

"What?" was the only response I could come up with. She just laughed and hooked her arm into mine.

"Come on, my little yellowbird. The sea is calling us. Best to not keep her waiting."

"So, WHAT GOIN' *on* with Alex? I want to hear all about it." My mother was grinning like a teenager and digging her fingers in the golden pink sand as the waves washed over us. A grin of my own split my face, and I turned my head to gaze at the sea, my mind drifted elsewhere, like the elevator.

"He's...really nice." I turned to face her again. She smiled slyly and placed a hand over mine.

"I already knew that, child. I meant how was your date? Did he like Oistin's? Did he see how much flying fish you can eat and run in the other direction? What did you do? Tell. Me. Everything." Her eyes were glittering in anticipation, and I was so grateful for these moments. I gave her a full accounting of yesterday.

We laughed about Paul and Nadine.

"They sound like good people. Remind me to talk to your father about adding their cruises to our roster of approved excursions."

She twisted her silver medical ID bracelet around her

wrist as I told her about making love with Alex on the boat and my confession to him at dinner about the other men I'd dated.

"I'd always felt sorry for poor little Rodney," she chuckled again. "And I'm sad you had to deal with those Johnnys at school, but I'm glad you found someone you can trust and someone who makes you happy. He sounds like a good man."

"Could you tell that to Dad?" I proceeded to tell her about Dad and Alex's mini-standoff last night, our argument that followed and our talk this morning. She smiled and patted my hand.

"Calypso, one of my specialties is my uncanny ability to convince your father of most things." She gave me a sly smile causing me to wrinkle my nose in disgust. A delighted chuckle bubbled from somewhere in her chest. "But convincing him that there is a man alive fit to date his precious little ladybug is something I think even I'm unable to do."

Tianna returned to the cottage to find Mum and me dancing to old Patra songs in the kitchen and laughing. She was telling me stories about sneaking out with my aunt Jennifer to go to nightclubs when they were teenagers.

I hugged and kissed her, telling her I'd see her tomorrow before writing two identical lengthy reminder post-it notes about Paul and Nadine's boat and leaving one on top of her tablet and one on top her morning journal where she'd be sure to find them.

ALEX WAS WAITING for me at the top of the cliff. He was leaning on the elevator's doorway. Our table was empty.

"Where's breakfast?" I asked.

"I'm looking at her." His face split into a wide grin.

"You better be kidding." I giggled as he scooped me into his arms and marched towards the suite.

"Calm down, Goddess." He kissed me as he climbed the stairs. "You'll get your eggs."

SIXTEEN

"*M*r. Wolfe?" Maggie's voice sounded like a distant buzzing as I watched Callie slip into her bikini in preparation for her daily trip to the beach. I'd woken up with her in my arms for the past three mornings and she was leaving a lot later than she usually did, thanks to me, but I wasn't sorry. I *was* sorry that I'd been neglecting work for the past couple days, but only slightly.

My goddess blew me a kiss and tip-toed silently past me on her way to the front door. The urge to grab her, pull her into my lap and kiss her until she giggled nearly took over, but I couldn't do that in front of Maggie. Also, if I stood up, she would see that I wasn't wearing any pants.

"Mr. Wolfe? Sir?"

I snapped to attention and turned to my laptop screen to see Maggie's concerned, slightly annoyed expression.

"Hey, Maggie. I'm sorry. Where are we on the Bellinger deal?"

"Sir, we weren't discussing the Bellinger deal. We were discussing the manufacturing issues with your factories in China. There have been quality control issues and rumors of employee mistreatment."

"Maggie, I'm not interested in rumors. We have eyes in Guangzhou and Shenzhen. What are they reporting?"

She eyed me warily, tucked her lips between her teeth and looked down.

"What?" I narrowed my eyes and leaned forward.

"Mr. Wolfe." She cleared her throat and continued. "I sent you those reports three days ago."

Shit. It had been a few days since I'd taken a close look at my emails. I tried to think of something to say to save face. This wasn't me. I wasn't this careless. A few small mistakes or one giant one could undo everything my grandfather built. I felt like I was in a tailspin. I was pissed at myself and annoyed at Maggie even though I knew this wasn't her fault.

"Sir," Maggie sighed, and her expression became motherly, something it rarely did since she worked for my grandfather and I would come to her desk and steal chocolates from her bottom drawer. "No one is happier than I am that you are finally taking a break and getting some much-deserved rest. For a while, I thought you were determined to work yourself into the grave like Mr. Wolfe —your grandfather," she added unnecessarily. Being called Mr. Wolfe still felt weird, but it was a moniker I relished and waited for my whole life. The title only made me bristle when it came from Callie. I never wanted to be anything but Alex to her. "But I'm concerned. You've been in Barbados for over a month. Maybe it's time you came back to New York. You don't have to come back to work full time, maybe just show your face around the office. Get back into the swing of things."

Her words were making my stomach contents churn, but of course, she was right. I needed to get my shit together fast.

"Mr. Widnicki assures me that everything in Barbados is being handled, so I could have your jet ready in the next few hours..." Her voice trailed off, and I met her eye. She and Matt had been talking, and I had a pretty good guess about the topic of conversation.

"Yeah, Maggie. Schedule a flight. I'll be at the airport in four hours. In the meantime, I'm going to look over the China reports. What's happening with Bellinger?"

"Okay, Sir. I'll get right on that." She seemed to visibly relax and continued rattling off things that I should have paid closer attention to. Meeting Callie and days that followed felt like falling down a rabbit hole. How long did I expect this to last? A much-needed vacation was one thing, but I couldn't stay in Barbados forever. My department head meeting was next week and I'd never missed one since I took over. Last week, I made ten-hour round trip flight to attend the last one. Callie would have to understand, I mean, she went to Wharton. She was The

Closer's daughter. She knew how things worked. Eighty-hour work weeks were considered part-time for me.

My call with Maggie ended and I pulled up the reports just as Callie came home.

No, not home.

Just as Callie came back to the suite.

She walked in quietly, checked to make sure my call with Maggie was finished before settling herself in my lap and wrapping my arms around her. Her face was serious, and her skin didn't carry the salty scent of the ocean like it usually did.

"How was the beach?" I asked, kissing her temple.

She answered me with a tight smile and shrug before saying, "Fine. How was your call?"

My pulse quickened at the thought of telling her I was leaving in three and a half hours. So, I deflected.

"Fine," I said, shifting her in my lap so her perfect ass cradled the erection that had appeared the moment I heard the lock to the door beep announcing her arrival. A mischievous grin spread slowly across her face, and she twisted herself to straddle me before cradling my cheeks in her palm. Her warm, soft lips covered mine, and I leaned back in the chair handing over control determined to forget that in a few short hours I would be leaving for New York. I told myself it wasn't goodbye. I would talk to her all the time. I would fly to Pennsylvania every fucking night if I had to.

"Hey." Her soft whisper pulled me into reality. "What's wrong?"

I looked into her pale gray eyes, so full of concern. This was the moment to tell her I was leaving, but instead, I said, "It's a work thing. There's some problems with a couple of our manufacturers overseas. I have to read these reports so I can figure out what the fuck is going on."

She leaned forward and kissed me again. "Can I help?"

"You want to help?" My brow furrowed in confusion. "They're a bunch of mind-numbingly boring reports. I don't even want to read them." My hand slid down her back and cupped her bottom.

"You know, my parents pay a lot of money in tuition for me to learn how to interpret mind-numbingly boring reports and I'm pretty fucking good at it. But if you think I'm not capable..." She pushed off of me, stood and walked toward the kitchen. This was not the way to leave things. She was used to feeling underestimated, and I'd insulted her.

"Callie, that's not what I meant." I followed her into the kitchen, and snaked my arms around her waist, pulling her into me. I ran my nose from the hollow behind her ear down her neck and across her shoulder, planting tiny kisses along the way causing her to moan contentedly despite being pissed at me.

"Whenever you're near me all I want to do is touch you, taste you, and inhale you. I don't want to think about work or meetings or reports. Plus, I've learned very early on to never underestimate what you, Goddess, are capable of." My words elicited a small giggle from her, and she spun in my arms to face me. "Let me show you how much I missed you this morning, then if you want, we can look at the reports together."

I lifted her cover-up, slid a finger under the elastic waist-band of her bikini bottoms and tugged them down. Her palms pressed into the edges of the countertop to steady herself before slowly lifting one leg. I lowered myself to my knees to worship at the altar of her heat, steadying her thigh on my shoulder and parting her tender labia with my tongue. So hot. So wet. So ready for me. I feasted on her as she moaned, her hips bucking, pressing herself into my face.

Callie grunted as the first orgasm ripped through her. Her knee buckled threatening to bring her crashing to the kitchen floor. My arms wrapped around her hips to steady her and I leaned back onto the cold tile floor. She repositioned herself, kneeling over me and grinding herself into my face as my tongue roamed and explored her delicious folds triggering another full body shudder from Callie before she slid back to settle herself on my waist. My erection was nestled between her almost bare cheeks, threatening to erupt as she leaned forward to kiss me.

"Had enough?" I asked with a sly smirk when our lips separated.

"Haven't you?" Her breath carried the scent of her arousal from our kiss, her chest was heaving, and my cock stiffened a little more.

"Never." I wrapped my arms around her waist and rolled her onto her back.

"Alex?" My heart skipped every time she called me Alex.

"Yes, Goddess?"

"Let's go to the bedroom. This floor is freezing."

SEVENTEEN

*C*allie was taking a post-coital nap wearing a satisfied expression that made me feel like a conquering hero when I sent Maggie a message telling her to delay my flight. The phone immediately pinged with a reply, but I didn't look at it. Instead, I turned to face Callie and watched her sleep. After what seemed like hours, but was probably a few minutes, her eyes opened, and she smiled at me.

"You creeper." She giggled.

"Guilty." I conceded. She kissed me and inched forward until our bodies were connected.

"Do you want to go over those reports now?" She raised her eyebrows expectantly, and the small glimmer of excitement in her eye made me want to make love to her again.

"You still want to do that?" I asked. She answered me by

sucking her teeth, narrowing her eyes and attempting to roll away from me. "Okay. Okay. I'll go get my laptop."

A wide, excited grin split her face. If staring at months of quality control reports and safety inspections made her smile like that, I'd fill this entire suite with file boxes.

When I returned with my laptop, Callie had pulled on one of my t-shirts. It was disappointing but probably for the best. Her perfectly formed dark brown nipples that tightened and pebbled at the slightest amount of attention would be too much of a distraction. I tossed the laptop on the bed, slipped into a pair of pajama pants and slid onto the mattress beside her. She twisted her hair into a bun and grabbed my computer. She clapped her hands and rubbed them together, still grinning.

"What are we looking for?"

"How do I know you're not some sexy corporate spy seducing me so you can steal confidential information about my company?" I narrowed my eyes before leaning over and kissing her nose. She giggled.

"This is from the man impersonating a hobbit in order to spy on my family?" She quirked an eyebrow at me.

"So you can see why I'm so suspicious," I said in a low growl before aiming a kiss at her neck. She pushed me away.

"If you don't trust me, I'd be happy to sign a non-disclosure agreement."

"I'll settle for a kiss."

"When we're done."

"Fine." I fake pouted making her giggle before recounting my video call with Maggie and pulling up the reports.

"Well, you obviously need to address the employee mistreatment first, so we should look at the inspections." She began tapping on the keyboard. I nodded. It's exactly what I would have done. One corner of my mouth tugged into a smile of admiration as Callie climbed out of bed, grabbed my tablet from the dresser and handed it to me. "There's a lot here, so we should split it up."

"Yes, ma'am."

We pored over the reports for a little over an hour when I heard Callie say, "Hmm."

"What?"

"Let me see what you have." She took the tablet and held it next to my laptop. "I thought so. Look at this."

The screens displayed inspections for two separate factories in two different cities done eight months apart reporting identical data.

"Fuck."

"Yup. And look here's another one." After a few keystrokes on my laptop and a couple of swipes on my tablet, she showed me another one. Two cities, two factories, identical data, four months apart. "I bet if we had more time we could find a lot more. The odds of this happening once are pretty small, but twice or more..." She raised an eyebrow at me. I nodded. There was a big fucking problem that would get bigger if I ignored it, no matter how badly I wanted to.

"Fuck, Callie. You're a genius." I grabbed her and kissed her, making her squeal. "How the fuck did you figure that out so fast?"

She narrowed her eyes and pursed her lips before saying, "Aside from being a genius who's pretty fucking good at interpreting mind-numbingly boring reports?"

"Of course." I smirked before I bracketed her waist with my hands and leaned forward pressing our lips together. A smile slowly spread across her face.

"Well, my mother would always say that if you didn't treat your employees well, they wouldn't do good work and that people who are too lazy to do their job properly are also too lazy to cover it up properly. I mean, look at this one. These figures are clearly for a facility half this size… What?" Callie noticed me gazing at her.

"Nothing. I've never heard you talk about your mom before."

Her smile faded, and she glanced away briefly before looking at me again.

"Well, my mum grew up helping my grandfather. He owned a restaurant and a small hotel; only four units. She got a degree in hospitality management and worked in some of the larger hotels and resorts while she continued to help my granddad."

"So, how did she end up owning The Sterling?" I asked.

Callie eyed me carefully and was thinking so hard I could almost hear the internal debate going on.

"Hey, you have access to a lot of privileged information about my company." I held up my tablet for emphasis. "I trust you. You can trust me. I love hearing you talk about your life. You never talk about your mom, and it makes your eyes twinkle, so I want you to keep doing it." I reached out and ran the pad of my fingertip down the bridge of her nose. She sighed and her smile returned.

"Well," she said in another sigh, "you are sitting in a very expensive engagement present."

I furrowed my brow in confusion, making her giggle.

"My dad came to Barbados on a short holiday, met my mum and didn't want to leave."

My eyebrows shot up my forehead. Callie's smile widened, and she continued.

"My grandfather didn't trust my father and didn't want them to date."

That old fucking hypocrite. I thought back to my conversation with The Closer after my first date with Callie.

"So, my dad bought her this resort as a way to assure him that if he did leave her, which he never did, she would always be financially secure."

"Did that win over your grandfather?" I was wondering what I would have to buy for Callie to wipe the shit eating grin off of Barnabas Sterling's face: a whole island? I'd do it in a heartbeat.

"No." She laughed. "But it softened him up. I think he knew he wouldn't be able to keep my parents apart. Of course, I helped. He loved being a grandfather."

Could this be the reason The Closer held on to The Sterling? It made sense, but the Barnabas Sterling I idolized my entire career, and the man who threatened my life for coming too close to his daughter didn't strike me as the sentimental type.

"I gave up everything for love once."

Was that what he meant? I couldn't imagine The Closer, my age, lovesick and trading his custom made Brooks Brother's suits for Tommy Bahama shirts. But wasn't that exactly what I was thinking about doing?

I hugged her closer to me and planted a kiss on the side of her head. Her arms wrapped around my waist and I felt her curls tickle my chest as she rested her head on my shoulder. A heavy silence filled our bedroom.

"Callie," I sighed. She took my cheek in her hand and turned me to face her.

"You have to go take care of this." She put her hand on my laptop.

I cleared my throat. "Yeah."

"Are you..." She looked away for a moment before her eyes slid back to mine. "...coming back or...?" She tucked a long curtain of curls behind her ear.

"When do you go back to Wharton?" I asked.

"School?" she replied with a mischievous smirk that made

me feel like I was tearing myself in half. The part of me that was Alex wanted to stay in this bed wrapped around his goddess with his nose tucked into her curls and inhaling her sweet, beautiful scent while counting the seconds until her next smile but Mr. Wolfe CEO had a company to run, a legacy to uphold and thousands of people depending on him for a paycheck. "In about a month."

"Come with me." It was a bad idea, but one born of desperation.

"I… can't." She seemed to consider it for a split second, but her face was serious, and I felt like she wanted to tell me something, maybe reveal another mystery about herself. "I can't leave my dad."

I knew better than to press her for more information. "Then I'll come back. As soon as I possibly can." I stroked her cheek, and she nodded. "I'll call you whenever I get a chance, and I'll text you all day long."

"I know you will, Mr. Underhill." Her face split into a grin that I was already missing.

EIGHTEEN

ALEXANDER

"*H*ey. Hey. Hey." I heard Matt yelling from outside as the crew was preparing to close the door to the medium size jet Maggie prepped for my return to New York. I was praying I could wrap up this bullshit in China in a day or two, without actually having to endure a twenty-eight hour round trip flight, meaning more time away from Callie. Usually, the thought of anything interfering with work pissed me off, but I realized the real reason I was pissed off because it ruined a perfect day in paradise with the perfect woman.

Callie used her lips, hands, and tongue to let me know how much she was going to miss me. Then I carried her into the shower so I could take her from behind, strumming her clit while she screamed my name, and also to conserve water. Finally, I was able to pack a bag but not without taking frequent breaks to partake of Callie's soft sweet lips and not without tucking my t-shirt covered in her scent into its own special compartment in my bag when she wasn't paying attention.

"Hey, Dick."

My head was so mired in missing Callie despite her being only a thirty-minute car ride away, that I didn't notice Matt board the plane and sit across from me. His taunt didn't have its usual ring of jocularity, and I was sure it was because he knew I wasn't happy about having to leave Barbados. I was hoping he thought it was because of China.

"What are you doing here?" My tone was harsh and accusatory, and I immediately regretted it, but I didn't apologize.

"Maggie," he said, ignoring my rude tone. "She thought you could use some back up on this China thing and this way I can attend the department head meeting in person tomorrow and save the company some money." He huffed out a chuckle, and when I didn't respond in kind, his lips formed a tight line, and he narrowed his eyes. He'd caught my confused micro-expression.

I'd totally forgotten about the department head meeting. For some reason, I thought it was next week, but it was tomorrow.

Tomorrow.

"All right," he sighed, deciding not to pull on that thread. "Catch me up with this China shit."

I was almost overcome by the impulse to make a snide

remark about Maggie telling him all he needed to know, but I knew that was childish. My sense of self had been slipping ever since I laid eyes on Callie. The three times I almost picked up the phone today to cancel this flight was proof. The Wolf, my corporate alter-ego had been sleeping, and it was time for him to wake the fuck up.

We buckled our seat belts, and the plane began to taxi down the runway. Matt leaned forward and listened carefully, totally focused on my words, as I went over the details of my video chat with Maggie and what Callie and I, found in the reports. I was careful to not let Matt know that Callie was the one that figured out that all of the reports for the last eight months or more were probably bullshit. Our relationship was a sore spot. He was probably just as relieved as Maggie was that I'd finally gotten my ass on a plane to New York, and probably showed up to make sure it was actually happening.

When I was finished Matt leaned back, balled up his fist and was tapping it on his chin, deep in thought.

"Peterson?" he finally asked.

"That's my guess. I have to figure out what kind of a mess this is, but when I figure it out, I'm pretty sure Peterson will have his hands dirty."

"If he's even that smart."

"Well, he's at least that stupid."

"So what are you going to do if it is him?"

"I'm gonna fire his fucking ass."

"You can't," he said. I furrowed my brow. I was the CEO. I did whatever the fuck I wanted. *"He's juiced in."* He did a bad impression of Don Rickles' character from *Casino*. *"His father's a senator. His mother works for the Department of Energy."*

"Okay, Billy Sherbert, what would you do?" I chuckled, and swirled a glass of scotch I didn't remember the flight attendant putting in my hand before taking a sip.

"Depends on how bad this is. Either give him a raise and job where he can't fuck anything up, so we stay in his family's good graces or if this is a total shit show, give his folks a heads up then throw him to the wolves. His dad will probably disavow him to save face anyway. Unfortunately, you can't fire someone for being an idiot."

"Yeah." I nodded and took another sip. The mouthful of dark liquid burned its way through my mouth and slid down my throat. That was the perfect solution, and Matt had come up with it so easily. He was hands down the smartest person I knew, maybe besides Callie. I offered to make him my COO when I took over, but he said I was too much of a pain in the ass to be my second in command, but he was anyway without the formality of a title. God knows I paid the prick enough, but he was worth every penny.

"Hey, man. You okay?"

I blinked and met his eye. "Yeah. I'm fine," I said parroting Callie's almost daily lie.

He sighed heavily and motioned for the flight attendant to refill our glasses.

"Alex," he said, leaning forward and clinking our glasses together, more out of habit than anything else. "This is what we do. This is what we were built for. We're not those white picket fence, two point five kids and a minivan kind of assholes. My dad worked all the time, and fucked anything that would stay still long enough, and my mother drank herself to death. Your grandfather cheated on your grandmother constantly and dropped dead two weeks after he retired out of boredom. That's us, dude. It ain't pretty, but that's what it is."

I knew what he was driving at, and though I wasn't thrilled about him using my grandparent's fucked up marriage to prove his point, he was right, but he was also so wrong.

It didn't hit me until his little speech. I'd always felt off my entire life. When I was a little kid, I would try on my grandfather's huge business suits patiently waiting for the day when they would fit me. Taking over Wolfe Industries felt the same way. I had some big shoes to fill, and every day I pushed myself harder and harder to be the man I thought I was supposed to be, the man my grandfather raised me to be and the man the world expected me to be. Seven years later, I didn't feel any different, but now instead of the suit being too big, it felt too tight. I was slowly suffocating, and Callie was my oxygen. If the role of CEO of Wolfe Industries was killing me, the role of Callie's lover, protector, confidante, and personal comedian was bringing me back to life.

"I don't know what this last week was for you," Matt

polished off his scotch and signaled for another, "but whatever it was I hope you got it out of your system."

Not a chance.

NINETEEN

CALYPSO

*M*y phone pinged for the third time when I finally opened my eyes and reached for it. The pillow my head was resting on was heavy with Alex's indescribable scent and the t-shirt I was wearing, which I shamefully fished out of the dirty laundry pile in a moment of desperation, carried his musky *fresh from the gym* smell. That was how much I missed him. I was sleeping in his suite when he wasn't even here, with my nose pressed into his pillow wearing his dirty clothes.

Damn, this was pathetic.

I slid the phone off of the nightstand.

MR. UNDERHILL: GOOD MORNING GODDESS.

MR. UNDERHILL: I WOKE UP MISSING YOU THIS MORNING.

MR. UNDERHILL: DID YOU MISS ME?

I smiled at the screen.

ME: YOU LEFT YESTERDAY. CALLED ME WHEN YOU LANDED AND BEFORE YOU WENT TO SLEEP AND TEXTED EVERY MOMENT IN BETWEEN. YOU HAVEN'T GIVEN ME A CHANCE TO MISS YOU.

MR. UNDERHILL: DOES THAT MEAN I SHOULD STOP?

ME: I DIDN'T SAY THAT.

MR. UNDERHILL: YOU ALSO DIDN'T ANSWER MY QUESTION.

ME: YES.

MR. UNDERHILL: YES, WHAT? I'M GONNA NEED A VERBAL CONFIRMATION, MISS STERLING.

I giggled.

ME: YES, ALEXANDER WOLFE, I MISS YOU

ME: A LOT.

MR. UNDERHILL: I CAN'T STOP THINKING ABOUT YOU. YOU'RE MAKING IT VERY HARD TO CONCENTRATE ON THIS MEETING.

ME: YOU'RE IN A MEETING?! WHY ARE YOU TEXTING ME? THAT'S NOT VERY PROFESSIONAL BEHAVIOR FOR A CEO.

I waited for his reply. A minute passed, then five. I was wondering if I'd gone too far and said the wrong thing before he replied after ten agonizing minutes.

MR. UNDERHILL: SORRY, I HAD TO GO BE A PROFESSIONAL CEO FOR A FEW MINUTES. (WINKING EMOJI)

Relief flooded my body, and I rolled my eyes.

ME: GOODBYE, ALEX. I'M GOING TO GET READY TO GO TO THE BEACH.

MR. UNDERHILL: WHERE ARE YOU?

I thought for a moment considering my answer.

ME: HOME.

That was a mostly truthful answer. Alex had the annoying but endearing habit of referring to his suite as our home as if we were a couple of blissful newlyweds. I also wasn't sure I wanted him to know I was sleeping in his bed, wearing his clothes and pining for him like a lovesick teenager.

MR. UNDERHILL: THAT'S A SHAME. I WAS IMAGINING YOU NAKED BETWEEN THE SHEETS IN OUR KING-SIZED BED.

MR. UNDERHILL: YOUR MANE OF CURLS, WILD AND DRAPED ACROSS THE PILLOWS. YOU OPEN THAT SINFUL LITTLE MOUTH OF YOURS AND SLIDE YOUR TWO MIDDLE FINGERS BETWEEN THOSE GORGEOUS FULL LIPS GETTING YOUR FINGERS WET AND READY.

As if he were texting me commands, I followed his instructions to the letter. The thought of Alex in a room full of people in business attire while secretly sending me all of his dirty innermost thoughts was making me hot and bothered. My legs parted, and my newly moistened fingers caressed my opening, hot and slick with my longing for him. My phone pinged again.

MR. UNDERHILL: YOU'RE PARTING THE CURLS ON THOSE TENDER PUFFY LIPS SO YOU CAN GLIDE YOUR SLICK FINGERS OVER YOUR ACHING SWOLLEN CLIT.

Mr. Underhill: You're using the other hand to caress those delicious tits. Pinching those tender little nipples imagining they were my teeth. I wish I was there to slide my tongue over those sensitive peaks feeling them stiffen under my lips.

I dropped the phone and my back arched as I made circular motions with my fingers satisfying the searing desire between my thighs, sliding my other palm over one breast desperately, my body aching for Alex's big strong everything. Whimpers and moans provided the soundtrack for my full body writhing until I sucked in a final gasp. Every muscle in my body was momentarily frozen after I tumbled off of the cliff I'd driven myself to with my frenzied fingers and Alex's filthy words.

My limbs felt heavy, my chest rose and fell as I drew in a deep lazy breath and my eyes drifted closed. The drunk, heady feeling washing over me was amazing. My skin shimmered and buzzed with a low electric current of satisfied pleasure, but it was a distant second to the real thing.

My phone pinged again.

I sucked my middle fingers into my mouth savoring the taste of my need, briefly considering sending Alex a picture of the aftermath of his text storm, but I knew better, and he would know I was in his suite.

Mr. Underhill: Goddess? Are you still there?

Me: Yes.

Mr. Underhill: Where did you go?

Valhalla. Nirvana. Paradise. Cinnabon.

ME: I WAS IN THE BATHROOM.

MR. UNDERHILL: (SMILING DEVIL HORN EMOJI) I DON'T BELIEVE YOU.

MR. UNDERHILL: SEND ME A PICTURE.

ME: NO PICTURES.

MR. UNDERHILL: COME ON. YOU TAKE SELFIES OF US ALL THE TIME.

ME: THAT'S DIFFERENT. MEMORIES ARE PRECIOUS.

MR. UNDERHILL: SO, SEND ME A MEMORY. (SMILING DEVIL HORN EMOJI)

ME: ABSOLUTELY NOT.

MR. UNDERHILL: (FROWNING EMOJI)

ME: ARE YOU FORGETTING ME ALREADY?

MR. UNDERHILL: NOT A CHANCE.

ME: WELL, IF YOU WANT TO SEE ME SO BADLY, THEN I WOULD SUGGEST YOU COME BACK TO BARBADOS.

I bit my lip and waited for a reply. How was it possible that I'd become so attached to someone in so little time? The feeling was exhilarating and terrifying at the same time. Every time we stopped texting, even if it was for a few minutes, I'd be sure that he would settle back into his life in New York and forget all about me. Then I'd get a message or a phone call, and I'd be flooded with embarrassing relief.

Experiencing disappointment at the end of relationships wasn't new for me, but Alex had the power to annihilate me. Despite my best efforts to keep him at arm's length, he held my heart squarely in the palm of his hand and all he had to do to destroy me was close his fingers and squeeze. My heart beat faster as the seconds ticked by.

MR. UNDERHILL: I'M WORKING ON IT, GODDESS.

I exhaled.

Ugh. Why had I been holding my breath?

I needed to get myself under control and go to the beach before it got too late. Mostly, I needed to get out of Alex's bed and out of his suite.

ME: I HAVE TO GO, BUT I'LL TALK TO YOU LATER?

Ugh. Why did I add a question mark?

MR. UNDERHILL: YES. YOU WILL. PERIOD. (WINKING EMOJI)

MR. UNDERHILL: HAVE A GOOD BEACH DAY, BEAUTIFUL.

Even though Alex had no idea what constituted a good or bad day at the beach I loved how supportive he was and how he never pushed me into giving him the information I wasn't ready to share.

ME: THANK YOU, HANDSOME.

ME: …

I typed another message. It was short. Just three words; ten characters, including the spaces. I deleted the text before I could tap the send icon, tossed my phone on the bed and started getting ready deciding that I'd kept the sea waiting long enough.

TWENTY

CALYPSO

*M*y body seized when I reached the edge of the stone path to find Tianna for waiting me. Her face was grave. Today would not be a good beach day. I sighed and forced my feet to move closer to where she was standing.

"How is she?" My voice was a shaky whisper.

"She was a little *confused* this morning." Tianna's words were gentle, but her expression betrayed her soothing tone. My mother was more than confused. Her best friend's eyes were heavy with worry and pity.

"Does she want to see me?"

Why was I still whispering?

"I think you should try. Maybe use the sunglasses."

I nodded solemnly and trudged towards the front door. The bell over the door jingled as I slowly pushed it open. Before I could reach into the entryway basket for my sunglasses, my mother whipped around and ran into my arms.

"Jennifer, thank God! I've been calling you all day." She held me away from her and looked into my pale gray eyes expecting to see my aunt's dark brown irises. Her face fell, and her arms dropped to her sides.

I stood rooted to the spot, quiet and searched her face for the faintest spark of recognition. After what felt like an eternity, she spoke.

"You're not my sister. You're my daughter, Calypso." She flicked a glance at the wall behind me.

I knew she didn't know me, but must have recognized my photo from the memory book she keeps by her bedside or from one of the photos hanging around the house.

She stood quietly, facing me as her eyes roamed over my face before she spoke again.

"You look exactly like my sister." She reached out to touch my face, but paused, raising her eyebrows at me.

"It's okay—" I stopped myself from calling her Mum. I didn't want to upset her any further. She caressed my face and sighed. Her expression was worried and exhausted.

"You look exactly like my sister, Jennifer, but you have your father's eyes." She remembered Dad. Despite my sadness, I was grateful for that. At least Dad might have a good beach day. "Where is my Barney? Did he come with you?" She looked to the door, most likely hoping my father would walk through it so she wouldn't be alone with this strange hybrid clone of the people she loved most in the world but didn't recognize. My eyes stung with tears and I blinked rapidly willing them not to fall.

"Your father wanted a little girl so badly." She smiled a kind sad smile. "And you are so beautiful." She had moved to stroking my hair. "I used to braid Jennifer's hair every morning before we went to school. We always said when we grew up and got married, we would have little girls of our own so we could braid their hair." She laughed at the memory in a way that made her eyes light up. "Can I braid your hair Calypso?" She called me Calypso, not yellow-bird, ladybird or her sweet child, but at least I was me. I swallowed the lump that formed in my throat and nodded.

Mum walked to her chair and sat. I retrieved the boar-bristle brush, the rat-tailed comb and the small jar of coconut oil from the bathroom. When I was home last summer, I counted three prescription bottles in her medicine cabinet. Today there were five. I slammed the cabinet shut and ran out of the bathroom. I handed the items to my mother and settled myself on the floor between her thighs.

"So, we've done this before," she said with a soft chuckle. We'd done this thousands of times before. Mum braided my hair the day of the meeting.

My encounter with Alex in the elevator was interrupted by a message from Tianna. After I left her, Mum had asked for me and wanted me to go back to the cottage. I had to take the long way to avoid the elevator, but she remembered me. She braided my hair and told me I'd be amazing in the meeting and she was right, I was. I wondered if the meeting would have gone the same if she was having a day like today.

Mum began massaging the oil into my scalp and humming the melody to "Yellowbird."

"I know you are my daughter. I know you are twenty-three. You attend Wharton like your father did. Your favorite color is blue because you love the ocean and your favorite food is fried flying fish." My mother sounded like she was reading a dating profile. "I know that because I read it in my journal this morning. I've seen videos, but they're hard to watch because I see myself doing things I can't remember. I also know you must be my daughter because my heart recognizes you. Does that make sense?"

I didn't speak, but I nodded with silent tears streaming down my cheeks.

"We didn't get pregnant right away as we hoped. We tried for such a long time, and when we found out about you, we fell to our knees, prayed and thanked God. Yes, your father prayed."

I jerked my head up, and she instinctively tapped me sharply on the head with comb making my scalp sting; the signal to keep my head still. Her words surprised me because Dad was never really religious, and his current relationship with God was tenuous at best these days.

"You were our miracle, and we knew it was likely you'd be our only one." She sighed, and I felt the tip of the comb slide down the center of my scalp as my mother parted my hair into two sections.

"You loved flying fish even before you were born. I would send your father to your gran's house almost every day to pick up the big batches she would fry up for me because I was craving them so badly. And you weren't a big kicker. You were a roller. You would just roll from one side of my belly to the other like you were swimming." She laughed again. My tears continued to flow.

"And those damned hiccups— tilt your head back, Calypso— you used to get the hiccups every day in the latter part of my pregnancy. They weren't painful, just uncomfortable, and constant. So, I grew to dread them. One day, you didn't get the hiccups, and I got worried. Your father told me you were fine. I insisted we call the midwife, who also said you were fine. My mother and the obstetrician both said you were fine, but I wasn't convinced. I made your father drive me to the hospital and just as we pulled into the car park, you started hiccupping. I never took those cursed hiccups for granted again." She let out a small chuckle and paused for a long time. "I remember that day so clearly. I can still feel the way my belly jumped. I never want to forget that. I always want to remember the way it felt to carry you inside me…" She was quiet for a minute, then she spoke again. "Oh Calypso, I'm so sorry I can't remember you. I'm trying so hard. I can see you as a baby. I can see the day when you lost your first tooth, but other parts…" She sighed, and I could hear the frustration in her voice.

Gulping sobs that I couldn't control accompanied my steady stream of tears. I spun on my knees wrapped my arms around her waist, pressed my face into her soft belly and cried. I felt selfish crying for the mother I was losing when my mother was losing so much more. I should have been more careful hugging her the way I did because I was essentially a stranger, but I didn't care. For a stupid, foolish moment, I thought the strength of my embrace could bring her memories flooding back or maybe I could keep more from slipping away.

I half expected her to recoil from my forceful hug, but she didn't. She wrapped her arms around me and stroked my hair. Was she comforting me because she recognized me or was she comforting me because my mother was the type of woman who would comfort anyone in pain because that was who she was and couldn't be forgotten? I didn't care. I just stayed locked in that silent, painful embrace as long as she would let me.

"Shh. Shh. Shh. Don't cry, little one." Her voice was soothing, and I wondered if she was imagining me as an infant. She began to sing in a low soft voice:

One day I prayed to the angels

as I sat in the sea

I asked them to please send me

a little baby to squeeze

We named her Calypso and

she's as cute as can be

She's clever like her dad but

She funny like me.

. . .

SHE SANG two more verses of *Calypso's Lullaby*, a song she made up to sing to me every night before bed, and I wondered how long she would be able to remember the words. My tears and my breathing slowed. My head rested on one of her thighs and I kept my eyes were closed as she continued stroking my hair.

"Calypso," she whispered. "Was I a good mother?"

I sighed, and a tear slipped past my closed eyelids.

"You *are* the best mother."

WE SAT TOGETHER in each other's arms until we heard the bell over the door jingle softly. I opened my eyes to see my father gazing at us, his expression unreadable. My mother perked up, her excitement palpable. She recognized him.

"Barney," she sighed. "I met our daughter."

"I see that, love." His eyes were sad, but he smiled at my mother.

"She's so beautiful." She was still stroking my hair. "She looks just like Jeje, doesn't she?"

"I'd say so." He took a few steps closer and settled into a nearby chair.

"Have you spoken to her today? I've been calling her all morning, and she hasn't called me back."

"Hmm..." was all my father said before giving me a pointed look.

It was time for me to go. He usually didn't come to the cottage until later in the afternoon, but I suspected Tianna must have called him.

I stood and faced my mother. Her expression was kind, but without the spark of recognition she had for Dad.

"Can I give you a kiss goodbye?" she asked. I nodded and leaned down. The two neat plaits she braided my hair into slipped over my shoulder and Mum flipped them back with an expert flourish of her hands. She cupped my cheeks and kissed them both.

"I love you, Calypso," she said. "I know that I love you."

I nodded again, afraid that if I spoke, I'd start crying again. Dad grabbed my hand and squeezed as I walked past him. His face was clouded with worry. He looked older, exhausted. If I were braver, I would stay in this cottage and we could face what he was about to tell my mother and her reaction together. But I wasn't and I couldn't. And he didn't want me to. There was so much he couldn't protect me from, but this was something he could, for now.

I DON'T KNOW why I went back to Alex's suite, but it was the most comforting place I could think of. If Alex were still here, I would walk in the suite, and his face would light up instantly lifting my spirits. He would ask me how the beach was, I would lie, and then he would hold me in his arms and pretend to believe me. I needed that so badly today, but he wasn't here. He was in New York, maybe for another few days, weeks or maybe forever.

The sheets were cool when I slipped between them. Alex's pillow was still heavy with his scent when I hugged it close and began to sob. I cried so much that I gave myself the hiccups which made me cry even harder. When my tears subsided, my body felt weak and heavy. I closed my eyes and fell into a deep sleep.

I SMELLED him before I registered his weight on the bed. Alex's indescribable, unmistakable scent invaded my nostrils before spreading through my body enveloping me like a warm hug. I opened my eyes to see him lying beside me fully dressed in one of his *made only for him* suits. He hadn't even removed his tie. A wistful smile adorned his face as he gazed at me the way a child looks at a sleeping kitten.

"You creeper," I whispered.

"Guilty." His mouth spread into a devastating grin making my body flood with warmth.

"What are you doing here?"

"This is my suite, Goddess, but I have to say the turndown service at The Sterling is definitely the best I'd ever experienced. Five stars." He winked, and I giggled. "What are *you* doing here?" He slid a fingertip gently down the bridge of my nose. "Not that I'm complaining."

"Claiming squatter's rights," I deadpanned, and he laughed. God, how I missed his laugh. Hearing it over the phone didn't come close to seeing his eyes light up and feeling his deep rumbling chuckle vibrate in my chest.

Alex lifted one of my braids and twirled it between his fingers before dropping it on my shoulder.

"I like your hair." His smile faltered when he saw my face fall. He slid his hand over my shoulder, pulling down the sheet. His eyes skimmed my body, and he saw I was still wearing my bikini. The sun had set meaning I must have slept all day. Alex's worried ocean blue eyes met mine. I wondered if he could tell that I'd been crying.

"How was the beach?" he asked, grazing my arm with his fingertips.

"Fine," I whispered before I felt a betraying tear slip out of my eye slide across my nose and down the opposite cheek. He climbed out of bed, stripped down to his tank top and boxer briefs, and slid between the sheets before pulling me into him and pressing my face into his chest just like he did in the elevator. His warm, soft lips pressed a kiss to the top of my head, and I fell apart sobbing in his arms. He never asked me why I was crying. He just held me until I stopped.

It took a very long time.

TWENTY ONE

ALEXANDER

ew York felt duller and dirtier than I remembered. I kept counting the minutes until I could text, call or video chat with Callie. I missed her scent, her touch, and her smile. I didn't only miss Callie. I missed Barbados; the smell of the sea, the feeling of the sand between my toes and the overall sense of calm. Everything about work irritated me. Now that I had some perspective, I realized how superfluous all the shit I did at the office was. I told myself I was an effective boss, but I was a tyrant. What was the point of paying recruiters to hire the best and brightest if I was just going to fucking micromanage them and spend every second of my life at the office?

Every second of my life was the office, until Barbados and until Callie.

I didn't get the same thrill walking into the skyscraper adorned with the five twelve-foot-tall letters that encompassed my legacy. It felt like a tomb. My father and grandfather had given their lives to this building, and I was next.

Matt watched me like a hawk. We devised a strategy for China and Peterson before calling team meetings. I pushed back on every option that involved me actually going to China. He invited me to dinner then a Yankees game, and I made a bullshit excuse that I doubt he believed.

Callie and I watched *The Desolation of Smaug* while we video chatted, and after I said goodnight, I stayed in my office and continued to work. I could've gone back to my apartment after a few hours, but it didn't feel like home. Any bed without Callie in it would feel too empty, so I sat at my desk working on shit I could've been doing on my balcony at The Sterling with my goddess in the next room.

Maggie found me asleep at my computer the next morning. She brought me a double espresso and laid out a clean suit without questioning me. I showered, changed and made my way to the department head meeting thankful that I remembered to charge my phone the night before, just in case Callie needed me.

I went out of my way to avoid Matt after the meeting, the same way I did after the meeting in Barbados. He was glaring at me the entire time, and I know he knew exactly what I was doing. I couldn't and didn't want to explain myself. Everything at the office was being handled. The world was still spinning, and I didn't give a shit about anything else except the life I left behind on that island.

I sent Callie a text after the meeting. She didn't respond, and I didn't think anything of it. She usually didn't take her phone to the beach and probably hadn't gotten back yet. I messaged her again an hour later. No response. I called her phone. I called the phone in my suite on the off chance that she was there and kept coming up empty. I waited for another hour and tried to reach her again before I walked into Maggie's office.

"I'm going to JFK. I'll be there in an hour, and I want the jet fueled and ready to go. Don't breathe a word of this to anyone."

She sighed and looked at me with another motherly expression.

"Please," I added. She pursed her lips, but one corner quirked into a smile as she picked the receiver of the phone on her desk and dialed.

"Go." She mouthed with a smile. I grinned at her, and she rolled her eyes at me as I backed out of her office.

Six hours later, I jumped out of the car as it rolled to a stop in front of The Sterling. I ran to my suite and let myself in. Callie's sandals were lined up by the door, and her phone was on the kitchen counter where she usually left it. The screen was lit up with alerts for all of my calls and messages. She didn't answer when I called her name.

The door to the bedroom was slightly ajar, and I looked inside to find her curled up fast asleep. The surge of relief that hit my body at the sight of her safe and in our bed was so powerful I had to lean against the door frame to catch my breath. With my bag forgotten on the living room floor, I kicked off my shoes and crawled onto the mattress beside her.

Something was troubling her. It was something that had to do with her daily trips to the beach. She was still in her bikini and wearing the same expression that she wore that morning in the elevator. I was again overtaken with the primal urge to wrap my arms around her and protect her, even though I had no idea why she needed protection.

And that's exactly what I did.

"HEY, CALLIE?" I walked out of the bedroom into the living before settling into an armchair that faced the kitchen so I could watch her make breakfast. She was in the mood to cook after she went to the beach and I came back from the gym. She wouldn't get any complaints from me. Everything Callie made was amazing, and I loved watching her shimmy and hum her way around the kitchen.

"Yeah, Alex?" She tilted her chin up, grinning at me and pinning me with her steel gray gaze. She was wearing one of her tank tops and a pair of my boxers. She'd rolled the waistband a couple of times to keep them from falling down, and it was so fucking cute. The semi-firm peaks of her nipples were visible all the way across the suite beckoning to be touched, kissed and adored.

"I got an interesting call from Paul."

"Oh yeah?" She returned her attention to the cutting board on the countertop.

"Apparently, The NADINE was added to The Sterling's list of approved excursions, so he and Nadine are booked solid for the rest of the season and had to raise their prices."

She picked up her head to look at me and grinned again. "Really? That's amazing."

"You wouldn't know anything about that, would you?"

Her grin pressed into a sly smile. "Well, I might have mentioned something to the owner of the resort."

"Yeah, well, now it's gonna cost twice as much to sail the most beautiful woman in the world around Barbados."

Callie chuckled and walked into the living room carrying a fork full of food with one hand cradled underneath the tines to collect any droppings.

"Oh, I think you'll manage." She slid into my lap and blew on the fork before holding it out to feed me something made from potatoes. It was delicious and spicy. "Good?" she asked.

"You tell me." I slid my hand around the back of her neck and pulled her in for a kiss. She wrapped her arms around my neck and pulled me closer parting her lips and caressing me with her tongue. After a moment she broke our kiss with a soft popping sound.

"It needs more pepper," she said licking her lips before she climbed out of my lap and walked back into the kitchen.

"Paul and Nadine want to give us a sunset dinner cruise to say thank you," I called after her. "You up for it?"

"Of course, but I thought you and Paul were going fishing?"

"Well, we were," I started, "but I decided I'd rather spend the day with you, making love, if you'd be okay with that."

A grin slowly spread across her face. "I would be very okay with that. I just hope Paul wasn't too disappointed."

"Nah. We rescheduled for next week."

Her head jerked up.

"Next week?" she asked as if it was a foreign concept.

"Yup. It's exactly like this week, but seven days from now."

She narrowed her eyes at me and shook her head. "I just didn't realize you would still be here next week."

"Well, I extended my stay for a month. They already charged my credit card, and I'm not a fan of wasting money." I smirked at her.

"And you're planning on staying until the end of the month?" She wasn't facing me, instead busying herself with the stove, but I suspected she was avoiding eye contact with me. I walked to the kitchen, wrapped my arm around her waist and swung her away from the stovetop.

"I want to stay this close to you for as long as you'll let me. I already left you once. I'm not in a hurry to do it again." I leaned down and kissed her.

"You were only gone for twenty-four hours," she whispered our lips millimeters apart.

"Really? It felt like a lot longer." I brushed my lips across hers again.

"What about breakfast?" she asked.

"I'm looking at her." I waggled my eyebrows.

"I am not wasting this food." She gave me a peck on the lips. "Go wash your hands and set the table."

"Yes, ma'am."

"Goddess?"

"Yes, Alex?" Callie inched her nude body closer to mine in our bed and draped an arm over my chest.

"You never told me how the beach was today?" I looked down at her.

She grinned up at me and I had my answer. "Fine. How was the gym?"

"Fine," I parroted her. "Do you want to talk about yesterday?"

I was going crazy every minute I spent away from Callie and I know she missed me too but I wasn't naïve enough to think the state I found her in when I came back to the suite last night was because she hadn't seen me for a few hours.

She shook her head. "No." She fixed her eyes on me.

"You know you can, right? You can tell me anything."

"I know." She planted a kiss on my pec and rested her cheek on my chest. "I will, but when I'm ready, okay."

"Okay." I kissed the top of her head and leaned back into the pillow. "As long as there's not another dude down there."

Callie laughed so hard she snorted.

"No, of course not," she sighed when her laughter died down. "There are two."

"Two, huh?" I tickled her as I kissed my way down her torso. "So I guess that means I have to work twice as hard to keep you coming back to me."

"It couldn't hurt." She giggled.

"Where are you?"

"Is something wrong, Matt?"

"Answer my question."

"I think you know where I am. What do you need?"

Matt had been texting me all morning and I was ignoring him, but when Callie went to grab a late lunch with her dad, to which I was expressly not invited, I called him back.

"What do I need? I need to know what the fuck is

happening to my friend and my boss, by the way. Did you forget you had a company to run?"

"How could I forget? My entire life is Wolfe Industries. I've been preparing to run this company since I could walk and I know what the fuck I'm doing. If I can't step away for a couple of weeks without the walls crashing down then I'm a shitty CEO, wouldn't you agree?"

"I know you slept in the office that night and haven't been to your apartment once."

"How the hell do you know that?"

Maggie.

"Maggie told me you didn't leave the building and I'm in your apartment right now and you haven't been here for weeks."

"Jesus Christ, Matt. Maybe *you* need a fucking break. And for your information, I didn't *sleep* in the office or did you forget China is thirteen hours ahead of us. I was on the phone all night, doing my fucking job."

"Are you with her?" he asked and I didn't like his tone. It felt threatening.

"Who?"

"The person you were texting instead of paying attention during the useless fucking department head meeting, which *you* insist on having every two weeks."

"You don't need to be concerned about her."

"I don't?" Matt chuckled incredulously. "Ever since you

met this girl you've fucking disappeared. Has it ever occurred to you that she's playing you, dude. Something's not right about this whole situation. Sterling and his daughter are way too desperate to hold on to that place but you're too pussy whipped to pay attention."

"You're out of line, Matt," I spit into the phone through clenched teeth. "And she's not a girl, she's a woman. Don't be a fucking caveman."

Matt scoffed, then was silent for a few seconds.

"Man, I really hope you do know what the fuck you're doing. I'm worried about you."

"Don't be. I'm good." I ended the call.

I was better than good.

I was fucking happy for once.

I was in love.

TWENTY TWO

ALEXANDER

*C*allie was waiting for me at the pier. She was wearing a floor length wrap dress with full billowing sleeves in a bright blue floral pattern. The wind was causing the skirt to blow open exposing one of her long shimmering golden brown legs. The stiletto sandals she wore accentuated the curves of her calves and thighs making me want to run my fingertips and tongue over every square inch of exposed flesh. Her makeup was similar to her look from the meeting, enough to enhance her beauty but it didn't cover her freckles. The exception was her lips. Her full pouty lips were covered in dark red gloss I imagined smearing with thumb. She'd taken out her braids, and her long curls were dancing in the sea breeze. She was fucking gorgeous, and even more than that, she was funny, intelligent, sexy, generous, loving, and mine. She was all mine.

She grinned as I approached her, looked at her watch and

crossed her arms. I checked the time. I was twelve minutes early.

That was the moment I decided she would never have to wait for me again, because I would always be by her side.

"It's about time you showed up, Mr. Unde— what?" Her brow furrowed at my expression and she smoothed her palms over her dress, "Too much? I mean we've never been on an official *fancy* date, and I wanted to look nice. Did I go overboard?" She tilted her head and chuckled as I continued to gaze at her, awestruck. "Okay, you're freaking me out. Please say something."

"I love you."

"What?" she whispered. She clearly wasn't expecting me to say that.

"I love you."

"Oh."

"Oh?" I chuckled at her adorable shocked expression. "I wasn't planning to tell you like this, but seeing you here, like this... I can't help it. I couldn't let another second to go by without you knowing exactly how I felt. I'm completely in love with you." I took one of her hands and placed it on my chest. "This is yours, Calypso Sterling. Every beat has your name on it."

Her eyes sparkled with unshed tears. She reached up and wrapped her arms around my neck, which was easier with her heels, and pulled me down for a kiss.

"I love you, too, Alexander Wolfe."

"Hey!" Paul called from the deck of The NADINE, "You gonna stare at your gal all night or get on the boat?"

Nadine appeared at his side and slapped him on the bicep giving him a look.

"I'm planning on doing both," I shouted back causing Paul to erupt in peals of laughter. Callie and Nadine gave each other pointed looks and rolled their eyes at us.

The woman I was in love with teetered precariously in her heels as I lifted her on to the deck. She gave Nadine a hug and kissed both her cheeks. Paul took Callie's hand and kissed it.

"That's a fine looking lady you got there, Alex," he grinned at me.

"The finest." I wrapped a hand around Callie's waist and planted a kiss on the top of her head.

"Well, I don't know about that, young man." Paul snaked his arm around Nadine's waist and pulled her into him, planting a kiss on her neck. Nadine pushed him away with an elated and flustered look.

"Go start the boat, you old fool." Her eyes followed his gait with a small wistful smile almost making her look girlish. Callie looked up at me with her eyebrows knitted together and her bottom lip poked out giving me an *"Aww! Aren't they so cute?"* look. I leaned down covering her mouth with mine, taking advantage of her expression to gently suck on that lip before she pulled us apart, remembering we were standing in front of Nadine.

When Nadine finally dragged her gaze away from her husband and turned to face us Callie gasped.

"Your necklace." She breathed. "It's so beautiful. Is it new?"

Nadine was wearing a delicate gold chain with a large diamond encrusted starfish also made from gold. It *was* beautiful, and I immediately decided that Callie needed one, too, but hers would be bigger. Nadine's hand flew to her collarbone covering the pendant, her girlish smile returning.

"Yes. Isn't it beautiful? I'd been admiring it in Cave Shepherd for months and then Paul surprised me with it this morning. He's been in such a good mood these last couple of days." Her eyes drifted to where Paul was steering the catamaran. I couldn't tell, but I was willing to bet money that under her glowing tawny complexion, Nadine was blushing and that she also shared Paul's good mood, but it had very little to do with jewelry or chartered cruises.

"So," she clapped her hands together, suddenly all business. "I made you a tray of fruit, crackers, and cheese. There's extra blueberries because I know you like those," she said. Callie gave my hand an appreciative squeeze. "A bottle of champagne is chilling. I'm going to go start your dinner."

"I'm going to help you with dinner—" Callie began and Nadine raised a hand to object, "—and then, you and Paul are joining us. I won't take no for an answer." She released my hand and marched off towards the staircase leading to the kitchen. She moved surprisingly well in the heels once she got her bearings. Nadine looked at me for assistance, and I shrugged helplessly before she narrowed her eyes at me and followed Callie to the other end of the boat.

I approached Paul at the helm. He handed me a beer and gave me a sly half smile.

"Thought you were leaving?" His half smile morphed into a full-blown shit- eating grin.

"Yeah, me too." I knocked back half the beer in two large gulps.

"She got you, didn't she?"

"Yeah," I grinned and nodded, "she did."

Paul guffawed. "I knew it. I told Nadine when we met you two, 'That boy doesn't know what hit him!'" He chuckled once more and clinked our bottles together. "She'll take good care of you. That's a good woman. I can tell."

"The best," I said.

"Well, I don't know about the best. You have met *my* wife?" He grinned again, and we both laughed.

"So how *did* you and Nadine meet?"

Paul grinned and took another sip of his beer.

"I used to work with her brother down at the shipyard. She was the most beautiful looking girl I'd ever seen, but she was a skinny little thing back then and mean as a snake. She did not fancy me. Every day when she would drop her brother off at work I would say, '*Good Morning, Nadine,*' and she would roll her eyes and drive away. One day, her brother forgot his lunch, and she came to drop it off. Now, I never ate much for lunch, a piece of chicken between two slices of bread with some pepper sauce. She took one look at my pitiful lunch, screwed her face up and walked away. The next day, her brother gave me a bag." Paul's face spread into a wide grin. "Inside was a container with peas and rice, curried goat and a slice of coconut bread. Best meal I've ever had." He laughed.

"So, she talked to you after that?"

"No," Paul laughed as if I'd made the most absurd suggestion," but," He held up an index finger and wagged it at me. "That's when I knew I had a chance."

We laughed again.

"So, I know what happens when you cross a Bajan woman. What happens when you try to leave one?"

"I don't know, man," Paul shrugged and took another sip of his beer, "I've never tried."

CALLIE AND NADINE emerged from the kitchen carrying our meals. Nadine must have been feeling nostalgic because it was rice and peas with curried goat. Paul was right. It was delicious. It was one of the best meals I'd ever eaten, or maybe it was the company.

After dinner, Paul pulled up the anchor and went back to steering the ship around the coast. Nadine shooed Callie and I away from the table refusing to our offers to help clean up.

I led Callie downstairs and carried her to my favorite room on the boat. I set her down on her feet and sat on the bed so I could admire her beauty. She stood between my thighs and cradled my cheeks in her hands.

"Say it again," she whispered.

"I love you."

My hand traveled to the sash at her waist tied into a bow, cinching her dress and accentuating her small waist. A small tug was all it took to unravel the sash and open her dress like a robe. Callie was naked underneath except for a tiny golden brown lace thong that barely covered anything and two flesh colored nipple covers that explained why I couldn't see the usual round outlines enticing me through her dress during dinner.

Not that I wasn't checking, constantly.

Her shoulders shrugged and shimmied causing the dress to fall away pooling into a puddle of silken material at her feet. She bent down to reach for the straps of her sandals.

"Oh no, Goddess. Leave those on."

SHE OPENED her eyes to catch me staring at her again.

"Hi," she whispered.

"Hi," I answered.

"Can I take my shoes off now?" She giggled.

"Maybe." I shrugged.

"You're going to have to rub my feet because they're sore."

"Don't threaten me with a good time, sweetheart."

Callie snort laughed. I sat up swung her feet into my lap and slowly unbuckled the straps of her shoes and removed them one at a time, kissing the tops of her feet and soothing the indentation marks of the straps with my tongue before wrapping one hand around each foot and kneading the soft flesh.

"Well, this makes it worth it," she moaned, flashing a lazy grin at me.

"Say it again, Callie."

"It again, Callie." She tucked her lips between her teeth before I started tickling the bottom of her feet making her scream laughter.

Almost two weeks ago, I could barely get this woman to crack a smile. Now, she was the funniest person I'd ever met.

"Come home with me," I asked, but I wasn't sure if I'd phrased it as a question this time.

"Home in New York or Home in Barbados?" Her face was serious. I considered her question for a moment.

"Home in Barbados," I said finally.

She tucked her bottom lip between her teeth and bit down trying to fight the grin that was threatening to overtake her face.

"Yes." She nodded. "I'll come home with you."

TWENTY THREE

ALEXANDER

hree weeks passed since the night I told Callie that I loved her and they've felt like they were from someone else's life. I postponed my department head meeting, indefinitely. Matt was still taking the news about The Sterling pretty hard, but I was sure he'd get over it. He'd come back to the island and was overseeing construction on the properties we'd already purchased.

I spent nearly all of my time with Callie. I couldn't get enough of her. When she was with me, nothing else existed, and when she wasn't, I feel like a part of me was missing. I used to spend my days trying to add zeros to my net worth and putting my name on buildings, now my primary objective was making Callie laugh and burying myself in her sweetness as often as I could. Every day I kept finding new ways to fall in love with her:

I loved the way she stuck her tongue out when she read The Wall Street Journal at the breakfast table wearing one of my t-shirts and nothing else.

I loved the way she always danced when she cooked, tossed salt over her shoulders whenever she spilled it and had a fit when I didn't do the same.

I loved falling asleep with my face buried in her curls and waking up with her long legs intertwined with mine.

I loved that she thought I didn't know that she sneaks into the bathroom in the morning, brushes her teeth and climbs back in bed like she'd been there all along.

I love that we argued about Callie being completely fine with putting my dick in her mouth but wouldn't use my toothbrush.

"That's different," she would always say, which was something she'd say when she was losing an argument, which I also loved, even though Callie losing an argument was a rare occurrence.

WE'D SPEND our mornings making love in the suite until I'd go to the gym and she'd make her mysterious pilgrimage to the beach. I offered to go with her a couple of times, but, as always, she wanted to go alone. I was curious, but I'd quickly learned to respect her privacy, and she always came back, so it was simply another one of Callie's mysteries. During the day she usually took me sightseeing around the island.

WE WENT to The Barbados Wildlife Preserve where I was robbed:

"Hey! That monkey stole my hat," I yelled.

"Babe, that monkey did you a favor." She giggled.

"I love that hat. That's a custom-made Panama!"

"Then, the monkey did *me* a favor." She kissed me. "It was a terrible hat."

WE WENT to Harrison's Cave where I was traumatized:

"Callie," I whispered roughly as our trolley bumped along the cavern trail, "you cannot honestly say you don't see it."

"Alex," she whispered back, staring straight ahead trying not to smile, "I don't know what you're talking about. Now could you please pay attention to the guide?"

"Callie," I whispered again, "you know good, and god damn well all of these stalactites and stalagmites look like dicks."

"Alex." She snorted with laughter while simultaneously trying to shush me. "You are the worst."

"I'm the worst?" I muttered while tickling her playfully. "You are the one who brought me to an underground cave full of dicks."

It was also in Harrison's Cave that I found out Callie had a beautiful singing voice. At one point in the tour, the guide stopped the trolley at the largest part of the cave and asked if there were any singers to test the acoustics. Callie surprised me for about the thousandth time since I've met her by standing up, taking a deep breath and belting out the most beautiful song I've ever heard even though I couldn't understand the language. When she finished, the entire trolley applauded, she took a tiny bow a flopped onto the seat next to me.

"What was that?" I asked her incredulously.

"Italian," she said it like she was telling me the weather.

"You speak Italian?" She grinned and shook her head.

"*Parlo un po.*" She squeezed her thumb and forefinger together.

"So what did the song mean?" She took my face in her hands and pierced me with her beautiful gray eyes.

"My darling dear, believe me, without you, my heart languishes." Then she kissed me.

She took me dancing at a place called St. Lawrence Gap, which was a string of restaurants and nightclubs, where she taught me how to *Wuk-Up*. I was a quick study, but I was looking forward to more private lessons, ones that involved fewer people and less clothing:

"You move pretty well. Where did you learn to dance like that?" She smiled at me as she moved her hips and I matched her rhythm for rhythm.

"I grew up in DC," I shouted over the thumping bass.

"You know," she whispered in my ear, "my mother always

says you can learn a lot about a man by the way he dances."

"So what does the way I dance say about me?"

"That I'm in trouble." She pulled me into a kiss swaying her hips.

———————

SHE TOOK ME TO MUSEUMS, a zoo, the racetrack, a cricket game—which I'm still confused by even after she explained the rules twice, and about a dozen other places. Everywhere we went she took a selfie with her phone.

I told her she takes a lot of selfies for someone with no social media accounts. She would always smile and say, "Memories are precious."

———————

I WAS WAITING for Callie to come back from the beach. I'd already seen her exit the elevator and now waiting for her to get to the door of the suite was excruciating. I felt like a dog waiting for their owner to get home from work. I fought the urge to run down the stairs, grab her and bring her home.

Finally, I saw her approaching the door through the peep-hole, and I ran into the living room, leaped into a chair and grabbed the paper, pretending to read it. I heard the lock beep followed by her footsteps behind me in the kitchen.

"Oh hey," I called nonchalantly, "you're home. How was the beach?" She walked over to me laughing and sat in my lap wrapping her arms around my neck, kissing me.

"The beach was fine." Then she gave me a clever smirk. "You do know I can see the shadow of your feet under the door and that paper is from last week."

I loved that she was definitely the brains of this operation.

I growled and scooped her into my arms and carried her into our bedroom.

She wrinkled her nose after I dumped her on the bed and leaned down to kiss her.

"Babe, you didn't shower after the gym did you?" I kissed her and answered her by growling. She was like a fucking bloodhound the last couple of days. Picking her up off the bed, I tossed her over my shoulder and marched towards the bathroom. I opened the door to the shower and turned the lever. "Alex, what are you doing?" She was trying to sound tough, but she was laughing.

I stepped into the shower with her still over my shoulder. We were both fully dressed. She scrambled out of my arms.

"You're insane," she screamed as she peeled off her clothes. I undressed and stepped closer to her. She reached up and kissed me. "You're still stinky, babe. Now, you're just wet and stinky."

I growled again in response and lifted her, pressing her against the wall of the shower as she wrapped her legs around my waist. I entered her in one smooth motion, and I was in heaven again. Her sweet pussy was as tight and wet as it was on the boat and I loved that it was all mine.

She unofficially moved in with me the night of our official *fancy* date. After a few days, we exchanged test results and decided to stop using condoms since Callie was on the pill.

"God, I love you," I moaned as I thrust into her. "I love you, Callie." She began to moan, and I knew she was close. I was glad because I wasn't sure how long I would last.

"I love you too," she whimpered. "I love you. I love you. I love..." She came loudly, and I followed her. I began to kiss her neck and shoulders and chest as her orgasm faded.

I set her down on wobbly legs, and we finished our shower properly, with plenty of soap at Callie's insistence.

"Alexander?"

"Calypso?"

"What are we doing?"

"Showering?"

"C'mon, I'm being serious."

I knew exactly what she meant because I'd been thinking the same thing.

"What happens when you go back to New York, and I go back to school?"

"Nothing happens. We figure it out. This thing is real. I

want to be with you, and I'll do whatever I need to do to make that happen. I told you on the boat. I'm not letting you get away."

"This feels amazing, Alex. It feels like a dream I never want to wake up from, but I know how much you love your work and I feel like I'm taking you away from that. I don't want you to resent me."

"The only thing I would resent is anything that takes you away from me. Now, stop this," I kissed her, "and hit that spot on my back." She giggled and squirted body wash on a washcloth and began to massage my back.

TWENTY FOUR

ALEXANDER

*W*e heard the distant jingle of her phone on the kitchen counter. "Ignore it." I reached around her waist as she was already moving to leave the shower.

"I can't," she laughed, "it's Dad's ringtone. It might be important." She grabbed a robe from the hook and swept out of the bathroom. I quickly rinsed off and followed her. I shrugged into a robe and sat in one of the armchairs. Callie settled herself in my lap and tapped the screen on her phone.

"Hello. Good Morning, Dad…

"Alex? He's right here." She winked at me, then her face fell.

"Leave? What? Why…

"No, Dad. He promised me."

She was looking at me with alarm and slowly rising from my lap.

"This has to be a mistake…"

She was silent for a long time and tears started to form in her eyes, and she was backing away from me.

What the fuck was going on?

I started to walk towards her and reached out my hand. She backed into our bedroom, closed the door, and the lock clicked. I could hear her sobbing on the other side of the door, I tried the knob and started banging on the door.

"Callie, let me in. What's going on?"

No answer.

I opened the sliding door to the balcony and ran to the glass door leading to the bedroom. My robe was open, and my dick was swinging for anyone walking past to see, but I didn't give a shit.

Callie had pulled on a sundress and was sitting on the bed crying into her hands, the phone beside her was silent. I pounded on the glass.

"Callie. Let me in." She jumped up when she saw me and headed toward the bedroom door. I sprinted back across the balcony into the living room and cut her off before she could leave the suite. I grabbed her wrists.

"Let me go," she hissed. This is the conference room Callie from weeks ago, the great white shark.

"I'm going to let you go," I began slowly, "but you have to talk to me. What happened?"

"Are you really going to pretend that you don't know?"

I huffed in exasperation.

"Jesus Christ, Callie. I don't know. I don't know!" I threw my hands up, and she used the opportunity to take a step towards the door. I blocked her again.

"You won, Alex," she said, and I was still confused. "You won The Sterling. You closed The Closer and his daughter."

Her last sentence felt like a punch in the face.

"Callie, you're not making any sense."

"Matthew Widnicki went to my dad's house this morning." She was using her slow, patronizing tone but at least I was getting some information. "He showed him pictures," her voice became choked with tears, "of us... in the elevator."

She steadied herself on the counter and sobbed again. After a few moments, she continued, "He said if my dad didn't sell The Sterling, he would publish them."

"No." I held up a finger. "No fucking way. Matt would never do that." After a second, I thought, yeah, he would. This is definitely something Matt would do. My next thought made my head pound.

It's something I would do.

But not to someone like Callie. A cheating prick who

didn't want his wife to divorce him and take half his shit was one thing, but never someone innocent like Callie.

"She has no idea what our world is really like or what kind of people we really are."

But why did Matt do this? "I told him not to pursue the sale."

"Would you stop, Alex? It's over. Is this part of the game; feigning innocence? Are you some kind of sadist?"

"Callie. This is the first I'm hearing of this. How could you think I would do this to you?" She turned to face me, and her eyes are red, puffy and shiny with tears. I wanted to hold her, but she wouldn't let me get close.

"Alex," her voice cracked as if every word was painful, "he showed my dad," she swallowed hard, "my bikini bottoms."

I feel like I've been punched in the chest. Before she'd uttered the next sentence, I knew I'd lost her.

"He could have only gotten them," she swallowed, took a shuddering breath and continued, "from you."

I left Matt alone in the suite the day of our first date. The bottoms were in my suit pocket. If I would have given them back to Callie when she asked for them or answered Matt's fucking calls.

Fuck. This was *all my fucking fault.*

"Callie." I felt my face grow hot. "Don't go. Please, let me fix this."

She shook her head, and the tears were still pouring from her eyes.

"You have no idea what you've done."

———

THE FIRST THING I did when she left was to check my suit pocket for the bottoms even though I knew they wouldn't be there.

I thought she might have a least listened to me if it weren't for those fucking bottoms. How was I supposed to explain how Matt got them when I didn't even know? How could I have expected her believe a word I said? When I set foot on this island my only goal was getting this resort and she knew that. All of that changed when I met her and I'd spent every minute of the last month earning her trust and her love. Then, Matt brought everything crashing down with a fucking triangle of black fabric. Now I have the resort and lost the only thing that I ever cared about; her heart.

The next thing I did was scream and punch a hole in the bedroom wall, which I immediately regretted. I chastised Matt for acting like a caveman, then I'm punching fucking holes in walls.

The third thing was to fly like a bat out of hell to beat an explanation out of my best friend and employee.

The driver had barely stopped at the former Shangri-La Resort & Spa when I leaped out of the car and ran inside. I marched up to the front desk.

"Matthew Widnicki," I demanded, the receptionist's face was impassive.

"Mr. Widnicki is in a meeting. Who should I say is…"

"Alexander Wolfe," I growled. Her eyes widened in shock and recognition.

"Mr. Wolfe, I apologize," she scurried around the desk, "I'll escort you myself."

I was taking long strides down the corridor, and she had to jog to stay ahead of me. She tried to make small talk but she was short of breath, and I was ignoring her anyway.

We reached the conference room, and she grabbed for the handle, but I was faster. The door almost flew off the hinges when I flung it open and filled the doorway glaring at Matt.

"All right, team. Let's pick this up tomorrow," he said quickly, never breaking eye contact with me before a dozen people grabbed papers and portfolios then rapidly shuffled out of the room. When the last one passed me, I slammed the door shut making the walls rattle. I stalked towards Matt.

"Look, man." He was holding his hands up but stood his ground. "I know you're pissed, but it had to be done."

I growled, launched at him and landed a clean punch right in the middle of his face.

"Ow!" he gritted through clenched teeth. "Motherfucker!"

He touched his hand to his nose and pulled it away seeing

blood. He narrowed his eyes, crouched and ran at me full speed, tackling me into the wall punching everywhere he could reach. I pushed him away and clocked him again, this time landing a blow on his jaw.

"What the fuck is wrong with you Matt? How could you do that? I told you to back off The Sterling." I shoved him.

"What the fuck is wrong with you, man?" He shoved me back. "You haven't been yourself since we got to this place." He spit out a mouthful of blood and wiped his chin with the back of his fist.

"And what the fuck are you still doing in Barbados? Don't say to help with the properties, because you fucked one up." He held up a finger, and my fist tightened in rage. "And you haven't been *here*. I can barely get a hold of you. Maggie can barely get a hold of you. Would you look at yourself? You look like a fucking sunburnt lumberjack. Who the fuck are you these days? You needed a fucking wake up call. I'm not gonna let my best friend ruin his life over a piece of ass he…"

I launched at him again. He wasn't ready. I knocked him off balance, and in an instant, I was on top of him. I had my fist cocked and was prepared to put it through Matt's face when security burst through the door.

"Sir," they addressed Matt. "Is everything okay? We got calls of a disturbance." I looked down at him. Two rivulets of blood were running from his nose, and red bruises were blooming on his face. I'm sure I don't look any better. I stood up, reached down and helped Matt to his feet.

"It's fine, guys." He waved security away. "Just a little disagreement between brothers."

When security left, we grabbed two nearby chairs, turned them right side up and collapsed into them. I winced and grabbed my side where Matt nailed me in the ribs.

"You fucked up Matt," I groaned. "You really fucked up."

"What's with you and this chick?" he asked. "Why are you willing to fuck up everything you've built for someone you've only known for a few weeks?"

I looked over at him, feeling the tears stinging my eyes thinking of the pain in Callie's face the last time I saw her, the pain that I swore I'd never cause her.

"I love her."

"What the fuck are you talking about, man? Love? Are you fucking kidding me? Did you listen to a word I said on the jet?"

"Yeah, I did. You were right. All of the shit you said was right. Your parents, my grandparents, the company… But I'm not happy, Matt. I'm fucking miserable. I thought coming here and meeting The Closer would help me find something…"

"Help you find what? What the fuck are you talking about, man? You're scaring me."

"Do you remember my parents?"

Matt sighed, fixed his gaze on me and nodded.

"They were so in love."

"I remember." Matt reached out, put a hand on my shoulder and squeezed. "I know losing them when you were so young was hard, but I still don't understand—"

"I found that with Callie. She makes me happy in a way nothing else has. It's like… she's what I came here for. Maybe I've been looking for her my whole life."

Matt brought his hands to his head, pulling them down over his face and leaning back in his chair.

"Matt, I don't expect you to understand what I have with Callie. I'm not even sure I fully understand it but what you fucking did…"

"What would you have done if it were me?"

"If you were my boss, I would have fucking listened when you said not to pursue the sale. As your friend, I would have talked to you."

"I tried, goddammit." Matt leaned forward and pounded the table with his fist. "Who the fuck do you think has been keeping things together? Maggie and I are running out of excuses. You've been gone for over a month."

I opened my mouth to contradict him.

"And no, I'm not counting the twenty-four hours you flew home, made a couple of fucking phone calls and half-assed your way through the department head meeting. What do you think will happen when the board finds out about this? Or the media? Wolfe stock would nosedive. Are you really gonna try put all this shit on me and not take *any* responsibility? The world doesn't stop spinning because you're *'in love'*" He sketched air quotes, "or whatever the fuck is going on with you."

"Matt. I'll admit it. I'm fucking up. But I can't lose her. I can't." I buried my face in my hands.

"Alex…"

Matt reached out to put his hands on my shoulder again. I shrugged it off, stood and walked towards the door.

"Alex. Alex! Get the fuck back here…We need to talk about this. Alex…"

Matt's voice faded as I walked down the hall. As I reached the end of the corridor, I heard the dull thud of what was most likely a chair being thrown across the room followed by Matt swearing.

I climbed into the waiting SUV, ignoring the shocked faces of my employees who hadn't even recognized me as their CEO. Shit, I didn't recognize myself anymore.

"Back to The Sterling, Sir."

"Yeah," I said, lightly pressing a tender spot on my cheek and checking it for blood, "take me home."

TWENTY FIVE

CALYPSO

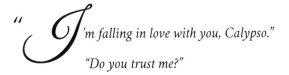*'m falling in love with you, Calypso."*

"Do you trust me?"

"I'll be gentle."

"It's important to you, and you're important to me."

"I'm gonna tell Matt to back off."

"If I say it, I mean it, especially to you."

"God, I love you."

"I love you, Callie."

I'VE BEEN CURLED up on my bed for the last three days heaving sobs and replaying every moment of the previous month of my life, wondering how I could've been so wrong about everything.

I ran all the way home from Alex's suite. I wasn't wearing

any shoes, and my face was puffy and swollen from crying. When I got to the house, I stopped dead in my tracks. Dad was waiting for me on the patio, just like he was the night Alex walked me home from the boat. He jumped to his feet when he saw me.

He didn't look angry or disappointed, but he seemed relieved to see me and also sad. I stood in the middle of the path, frozen in shame with tear-stained cheeks. He ran out to meet me and wrapped his arms around me.

"Oh, Bug," he sighed, "It's gonna be okay." He wasn't even upset with me, and he should've been. I should've been smarter than this. I should have protected us. I began to sob into his chest.

"Daddy, I'm so sorry."

He kissed the top of my head.

"This is all my fault, Calypso," he sighed, "I never should've gotten you involved in this, with these kinds of people; people like me."

The idea that my dad thought that this was his fault made me feel even worse. He brought me inside. I showered Alex off of me, slipped into a pair of pajamas and collapsed onto my bed crying. I hadn't left.

Alex had shown up at our door every day, begging my dad to let him in and screaming my name. I went to the window the second day and peeked through the blinds so he couldn't see me. He looked terrible. His face was bruised, and he looked like he'd been crying. I had the smallest impulse to go to him. A part of me still missed him and didn't want to believe that he was lying to me, but there was no other explanation.

On the third day, this morning, Dad finally said something to make Alex go away, but he never told me what it was.

———

"Calypso," he called from my doorway, "you need some sun."

I sniffled and pulled the covers over my head.

"Why don't you go to the beach? It's been three days."

"I can't."

"Yes, you can," he retorted, "that lift isn't the only way to get to the beach." Just the mention of the elevator was enough to send a fresh wave of tears sliding down my face into my pillow.

"I know," I sobbed, "I just don't think I can face her after what I've done."

"Oh, Bug," he sighed before he sat on my bed and patted my hip through the blanket. "She wants to see you. Were you planning on going back to school without saying goodbye?" Honestly, the thought had crossed my mind.

"Of course not," I muttered.

"Well, today's the day." He pulled back my blankets and threw open my shades. The cool air stung and the bright light was blinding. "And don't think I didn't notice that you haven't been eating. The last thing I want is for you to get swept out to sea. Remember what your mother always says: *the ocean…*"

"*…ain't got no back door,*" we finished in unison. We both smiled. It was the first time I'd smiled in days, and it felt strange.

"Get washed up, get dressed and I'll make you some eggs and toast." He tapped my door frame with his knuckle and headed to the kitchen. The thought of food made me feel sick, and I hadn't had an appetite since I'd been home; Dad's home, not the home I shared with Alex.

I stood under the hot stream of the shower and cried. I pulled on a bathing suit, then a cover-up and cried. Everything reminded me of Alex. I missed him so badly it made me cry, then I remembered what he did, and I'd get so angry at myself for missing him that I cried even harder.

Dad placed a plate of eggs and toast in front of me when I sat down at the table. The bright, orange, gelatinous yolks wiggling on the plate made me feel even more nauseated, and I pushed them away.

"Calypso," my dad pleaded, "please take a bite of something."

I obliged by nibbling on a corner of toast and washing it down with a sip of orange juice.

"Thank you. Do you want me to go with you? I was going to go later today, after a meeting." The word *meeting* made my stomach lurch.

"No, I can go alone," I mumbled, "Dad, what if he comes back?"

My dad sighed and his face set.

"I had a word with him this morning." He wasn't looking at me, but swirling the toast around in his yolk. I swallowed a lump that formed in my throat and tried not to look at it. "He won't be back. You'll be fine."

I nodded, trying to cover the tiny kernel of disappointment by drowning it in relief. I honestly didn't know what I would do if I saw Alex again. I wasn't sure I would be strong enough to resist him, but I was still so angry.

Dad was able to coax me into eating more toast, then a few blueberries and finally drinking a half a cup of tea. I actually did start to feel better, a little bit.

———

I STEPPED ONTO THE PATIO, and the sun hit my face. I looked to my left and saw the main building in the distance. On the other side of it were the luxury guest suites and possibly, in one of those suites was Alex.

I had a sudden flash of a memory of the beach elevator doors opening on Alex sitting at our table drinking a coffee. His face broke into a wide grin. He jumped up from the table and scooped me into his arms kissing me. In the next flash, he sat me on the kitchen counter, laying me on my back and making a joke about missing breakfast before unwrapping me like a Christmas gift, covering my quivering core with his mouth and devouring me to climax. The memory dissolved, and I wiped away a fresh wave of tears with the heel of my hand.

I turned to my right and walked toward the beach. It was definitely a lot longer than taking the elevator, and I probably should have taken one of the golf carts, but the walk gave me time to think, and the sun was energizing.

I was finally stomping down the hill where the cliff meets the beach before walking up the rocky path to the cottage. I was met outside by Tianna. She gave me a pitying smile and a deep squeezing hug that told me that she knew. She was also holding two towels, so she was sure I wouldn't be taking the elevator.

"How is she today?" I asked when she finally released me.

"Today is a good day," she smiled, "and she's been asking for you. Go on inside."

I stepped into the cottage, and she was sitting in her favorite chair rocking to The Merrymen playing on her stereo. I stood in front of her waiting for her to notice me. She turned her head slowly, and her face lit up upon seeing me.

"Calypso. My baby. I've missed you." She rose from the chair and bounded across the room and squeezed me into a hug. I returned her embrace, and my tears of sadness were replaced by tears of relief because today I was Calypso and she was having a good day.

"Hi, Mummy," I sobbed into her shoulder. I really needed my mother today. She released me from our hug, took my face in her hands and kissed my cheeks.

"My lovely little ladybird, it's going to be all right." She squeezed my hand and pulled me towards the door. "To the sea," she commanded.

We strolled to the shoreline, waded into the water up to our thighs and sat down, letting the waves wash over us. We were quiet for a few minutes when Mum reached for my hand.

"Your father told me what happened." Her face was serious, but like Dad, she didn't seem upset or disappointed.

"He told you," I looked down at my hand, letting the warm wet sand slip through my fingers of the hand my mother wasn't clutching, "everything?"

"You know your father can't keep secrets from me." She was laughing, but I couldn't join her.

"Mum, I'm so sorry," I sighed, triggering a fresh wave of tears, "I wanted to help, but I ended up ruining everything."

"Sorry for what, my dear," she smiled, "falling in love?"

"But it was all a lie," I sobbed.

"Was it?" she asked, and I looked at her incredulously. "Calypso, I saw the way you looked at him in those photos."

I opened my mouth to protest.

"And I saw the way he looked at you."

I closed my mouth and stared at her.

"Your father still looks at me that way." She smiled a

devilish smirk and looked toward the elevator. "You know, your father and I made some memories of our own in that lift."

"Ugh, Mum," I groaned. I loved hearing stories about Mum and Dad falling in love, but with fewer details. She threw her head back laughing.

"Where did you think you came from?" She shoved me in the shoulder. "The stork?"

"I don't need to hear this," I moaned, even though it provided a temporary reprieve from my own tortured thoughts.

"Your father tells me Alex has been coming by the house asking to talk?"

"Yeah, Dad finally made him go away today."

Mum's face spread into a grin, and she threw her head back laughing again. I started to worry and wondered if I should call Tianna before her laughing began to subside, and she sighed, wiping away tears.

"Mum, are you okay?"

"Did you know," she was still chuckling, "your grandfather chased your father away from our house," she pointed behind us at the cottage, "with a shotgun."

My eyes widened.

"He told him he didn't want any White men sniffing around his daughters!" She broke in more peals of laughter.

"Granddad did?" I asked incredulously. She nodded, her shoulders shaking and her face full of mirth, "but Granddad was a White man." I said. We both burst out laughing.

"I know that child," she said, still laughing, "I guess he thought he knew something about White men that Jennifer and I didn't. Of course, he didn't have to worry about that where Jennifer was concerned." Her laughter faded to a wistful smile, and I wondered if she was thinking about Aunt Monique. I hadn't seen her or spoken to her since she moved back to France last year. We were close and though it made me sad, I understood that everyone grieved in their own way.

Mum took my chin in her hands and turned me to face her. "But it didn't work. Your father would not be discouraged and based on what you and your father tell me about him; I don't think Alex will either."

"What did Dad tell you about him?"

"That he's clever, cocky and arrogant," she smiled, "so he reminds him of himself."

"He said that?" I was shocked. She shook her head smiling.

"He didn't have to." The wistful grin returned. "I remember your father back then."

I hoped she wasn't thinking of the elevator.

"But, Mum," I started to feel tears springing to my eyes again, "The Sterling—"

"—is a place. My heart is where ever you and your father

are. My mind, well…" She shrugged and planted a kiss on the side of my forehead.

"But what if it gets worse?" I felt more tears spilling down my cheeks, and she sighed.

"Calypso, it will do whatever it's supposed to do, whenever it's supposed to do it. Sitting here crying about it isn't going to help." She began to push herself to her feet. I jumped up to help her. "Now, let's walk. The doctors say it helps and you know I like to look good for your father." She patted her hips, and I groaned, rolling my eyes before we strolled along the beach.

I LEFT for Pennsylvania the following day. I visited Mum again before I went to the airport, but I wasn't Calypso, I was my Aunt Jennifer. Mum braided my hair and told me the story about her first kiss with my dad like it happened the day before because for her it had.

Dad arranged for a private plane, and while I usually don't mind flying commercial, I was grateful for the peace and quiet. In the car ride from the airport to Wharton, I kept feeling a sense of impending dread. I didn't want to be there. My heart was in Barbados in every sense of the word.

I wondered if Alex ever went back to New York.

I wondered if Mum was having a good day.

I wondered about the fate of The Sterling.

I wondered about my dad, juggling everything on his own.

I wondered how I would ever focus on school with everything else going on.

MY FIRST WEEK back was hell. I thought my rigorous academic schedule would be exactly what I needed to help me get over Alex but I couldn't concentrate on anything. I cried whenever I was alone. My student advisor was the first to point out that I didn't look well. She insisted that I see a doctor. I initially refused, then relented when, after fainting in her office, she threatened to call my father. Apparently, I wasn't the only graduate student to ignore the warning signs of stress with dire consequences, and she didn't want to take any chances. She also *strongly recommended* that I not return to class until I was cleared by the physician, which I knew was less of a recommendation and more of a threat.

I made the appointment for the next day. The sooner I placated her, the sooner I could get back to my version of normal. I knew what was wrong with me. I wasn't eating or sleeping. I was dehydrated from crying, and I was pretty sure I'd never be happy again.

I was suffering from a broken heart.

TWENTY SIX

ALEXANDER

I haven't seen Callie for almost three weeks. I honored my word to her father to leave her alone and let her decide when or if she wanted to see me. Every day that promise was harder and harder to keep.

I slept on Callie's side of the bed every night. I refused to let room service clean the room, and it was starting to show. She was everywhere in the suite, even though she'd been gone for weeks. Her toothbrush was still on the bathroom sink. Her shampoo was still in the shower. Her shoes were still neatly lined up by the front door. Whenever I'd find myself lasting five minutes without thinking about her, I would find one of her long curly hairs. I'd made love to her in every inch of this place, and I could feel her everywhere.

I hadn't been to the gym since the day she left, and every morning, I sat on the balcony staring at the elevator for hours, hoping one day the doors would slide open and she'd come striding through them.

THERE WAS a knock on my door. Callie had a key, and I hadn't ordered room service. There was only one person it could be, and I wasn't sure I wanted to see him. Nevertheless, I walked to the door and opened it.

"Hey, man," Matt said in a low voice. "Can I come in?"

He walked past me into the kitchen as I took a step back to let him pass. He dropped a couple of envelopes on the kitchen counter and began to make coffee. The smell was energizing, so I went to my bedroom and put on a t-shirt and pair of shorts. A mug of coffee was waiting for me on the countertop when I reentered the kitchen.

Matt spoke first.

"I brought some papers for you to sign."

"Why didn't Maggie messenger them?"

Matt's face set and his eyes flashed momentarily.

"Because I told her I'd deliver them to you. She's really worried about you and so am I. We keep waiting for you to snap out of whatever this is but you haven't. How long do you think you can keep this up? When's it gonna end?"

"Today."

He looked at me in confusion.

"I've been giving this a lot of thought. I still love Callie. I probably always will even if I may have lost her forever, but this isn't her fault. It's mine. Running Wolfe Industries was my birthright. I thought it was what I wanted, but now I realize that it's what my grandfather wanted and he died miserable and alone. I definitely don't want that." My thoughts briefly drifted to Callie and the prospect of never touching her or hearing her laugh again. I brought the coffee cup to my lips. "I was using Callie to avoid admitting the truth to myself, to you and Maggie, to the world."

"What are you saying, Alex?"

"I'm saying, I don't want it. Deep down I don't think I ever did. I'm saying you should have it."

Matt nearly choked on his coffee.

"What?" he spluttered between coughs.

"You should run the company. I'm stepping down."

"You're out of your fucking mind." He slammed the mug down so hard on the countertop it shattered spraying hot coffee all over the kitchen. "It hasn't even been a month since…" He didn't finish his thought, but I knew what he was thinking: *since Callie left me.* "You're talking about your whole fucking life. You're really gonna sit there and tell me this…" He caught my eye, *"woman* has nothing to do with this." Matt was flinging the coffee off of his hand. I grabbed a dish towel and threw it at him.

"Something was always off, Matt. Callie just helped me realize what it was. This was inevitable. It just happened sooner than I thought."

"And she asked you to give up your company for her?" Matt was using the dish towel to sweep the broken mug shards in the trash can.

"No. She doesn't know. I didn't know I was actually gonna go through with it until you showed up." Callie would never ask me to give up anything for her. That's why she was worth giving up everything.

"So what are you going to do if she doesn't take you back?"

Callie forgiving me was unlikely. That didn't mean I wouldn't try for as long as took, but I didn't step down for her.

"Matt, for the first time in my life, I can do whatever I want."

He just stared at me for a minute then he spoke.

"I'm not going to pretend I understand what's happening between you and Calypso Sterling," he said. My chest clenched at hearing her name, "but I clearly misread the situation and maybe I jumped the gun with the pictures."

That was a fucking understatement.

"Matt, Callie is brilliant. It took her less than an hour to figure out what Peterson was doing in China."

"You let your girlfriend read—"

"Yes, I did." I glared at him. "She graduated from Wharton with honors. She speaks Italian. She's a year away from getting her MBA. Do you know what would have happened to her if you published those pictures? You would have ruined her life. For a fucking property."

"I knew Sterling would fold. Those pictures would have never seen the light of day. Did you forget you were in them too? *Wolfe's CEO disappears for a month before being photographed fucking in an elevator.* The headline writes itself. Do you have any scope of the fucking mess you're making? Now you want to walk away."

"Matt," My frustration was getting too difficult to control. "Stop thinking about the company. Callie is a person, not a pawn. I'm a person, not a fucking institution."

"What about your thousands of employees? Are they people?"

"Yeah. That's why you should lead them, not me."

"Alex, you're a good CEO."

"Yeah. I am. When my grandfather stepped down, he told me that a good leader knows when it's time to pass the mantle. I proud of my time at Wolfe but I'm done. Whether or not Callie takes me back, it's over."

"Alex—"

"I've made up my mind, Matt. If you don't want it, I'll call a headhunter, but I'm done. I'd like it to be you, and I know my grandfather would have agreed."

He just stared at me for second before nodding this head.

"I have one condition."

Matt tilted his head and glared at me, but he didn't speak.

"You have to keep Maggie."

His face spread into a wide grin, and he chuckled.

"Of course. She knows that place better than either one of us. Does she still keep that candy in her desk?"

"Bottom left drawer."

We smiled. Matt and I were still miles away from being okay, but this a small step in the right direction.

"Okay. I'll have my lawyers start the process." I slapped him on the bicep. "Now, what do you have for me to sign?"

TWENTY SEVEN

CALYPSO

The doctor walked into the exam room smiling.

"All of your tests are normal, Callie."

I was still staring at her in disbelief.

"I'm aware of your mother's condition and while it can be hereditary. I don't think we should be concerned now."

I blinked.

"But you are under an incredible amount of stress, and that's a problem. You need to get that under control ASAP. Have you considered taking some time off from school?"

I shrugged.

"You should."

She nodded, then I nodded.

"I'm not going to sugar coat this. Continuing the way are

could have very dire consequences. It's too much. You need to focus on your health. I'm *strongly* recommending you take some time off from school." She tilted her head down to glare at me with eyebrows raised.

I nodded again in agreement. Her expression softened.

"Good. Now, I'm going to write you a prescription. You take two of these with breakfast."

She lowered her eyes at me.

"Eat breakfast. Every day."

I nodded again.

"I'll see you in a few weeks, and I expect you to be more relaxed."

I didn't see how that was possible, but I guessed taking time off from school was a step in the right direction, so I nodded again. I got up and walked towards the door to the exam room.

"Wait. Don't forget this."

She handed me a slip of paper.

———

I LEFT the Doctor's office and climbed into the back of the waiting SUV.

"Back to your apartment, Ms. Sterling?"

"No, take me to the beach house."

I DIDN'T DROP out of school. I was sure that if I took a few days at the shore to think and regroup, I could figure out a way to make sense of everything and get myself back on track. A few days turned into nearly three weeks, and I had to make a decision about school the next day or two. I still had a lot on my mind, but I think my doctor would be proud of the strides I was making in reducing my stress. I slept as late as I wanted and whenever I felt like it. Breakfast became a priority, and I was grateful to be able to eat eggs again without getting nauseated. My black tea was traded for decaf herbal varieties. I bathed in the ocean every morning and took long walks. My business textbooks and The Journal were traded for the growing stack of romance novels procured during my almost daily visits to the local library.

The book I was two-thirds of the way through was spread open on my lap. I was curled up in the large armchair in my living room, my legs tucked under me and covered in a blanket. The tip of my tongue was protruding through a corner of my lips as I read, finally coming to the crucial part in the story when the prince discovers that the spoiled, stuck up princess he was being forced to marry and the rogue bandit robbing aristocrats to feed the poor with whom he'd shared a mysterious night of passion, were none other than the same person.

The knock on the door startled me, and I was jolted into the present. I'd never had a visitor other than the house's owner for maintenance purposes, but they always called first. My next thought that was that it could be Alex, making my stomach drop, but I quickly dismissed that. My father would never tell Alex where I was. I approached the door cautiously to reveal my mystery visitor. It was the last person I'd expected.

———

"I NEED TO TALK TO YOU," Matthew Widnicki called through glass pane of the window of my front door. My flesh burned with anger from head to toe. I'd never hated a person before. I'd thought I had until this moment but seeing Matthew darkening my doorstep induced a feeling of intense dislike I'd never felt before. With one action this man had swooped into my life and taken away everything I loved, everything that made me feel safe. Now, he was here, standing on my front porch after having taken away my last haven, this beach house.

The white-hot rage consumed me. I wanted to hurt him. I wanted *him* to cry *himself* to sleep every night. I wanted him to feel every bit as guilty, hopeless and angry as I felt. Mostly, I wanted to pick up something heavy and hit him with it…repeatedly.

This was doing nothing for my stress, so I took a step back from the door, closed my eyes and took three calming breaths.

Matthew was waiting as I approached the door. Our eyes met. His eyes were also blue, but they were paler and not the vibrant ocean blue of Alex's. He was eyeing me, no doubt expecting me to welcome him into my home and offer him a cup of tea after he destroyed my life.

"Go away," I said and shut the curtain. I turned and walked to the sitting room foolishly thinking that it would be enough to make him leave so I could resume reading and not spending the rest of the day obsessing about how he found me in the first place. He followed me, knocking on the window and shouting.

"Please, I really need to talk to you."

Now he was begging, and it ignited a tiny flicker of satisfaction. I closed the curtain on his expression of increasing frustration. He moved to the next window.

"It's about Alex," he said. Those words made me pause. Was Alex hurt? Why was he telling *me*? If something bad happened to Alex, my father would have called me. Obviously, Matthew couldn't be trusted.

And neither could Alex, a much smaller voice in my head added.

I closed that curtain. Matthew's exasperated scowl appeared in the next pane of glass and disappeared again as I yanked the next curtain across the rod. We moved this way around the perimeter of my house, Matthew's pleas becoming more frustrated and my patience wore thinner as my house grew darker.

The last nerve that Matthew was dancing on finally snapped once we ended up on the inside and outside of my kitchen when he had the audacity to try to turn the knob on my back door.

"Are you out of your fucking mind?" I whipped around to glare at him crossing my arms.

"I'm not leaving until we talk." The fierce determination in his face reminded me of Alex, though not nearly as attractive. Not that Matthew wasn't handsome, but I got feeling if you tugged hard enough on his too perfectly chiseled features, his face would slide off to reveal a giant lizard, like in that Sci-Fi TV series from the 80's my dad loved. Thinking of Dad only made me angrier.

"Are you fucking kidding me? We don't have a damn thing to talk about. I can't believe you have the nerve show your face at my house. How did you find me anyway? Did Alex send you? Didn't have the balls to face me himself after what…" My voice trailed off at Matthew's confused expression. He was staring past me with his eyes narrowed. I followed his line of vision to the refrigerator and the small piece of paper my doctor gave me at my last visit. It was attached to the upper freezer door, held in place with a *Welcome to The Jersey Shore* magnet. All of the blood drained from my face, and I let out a deflating sigh.

Shit.

I turned back to Matthew. His eyes slowly slid back to mine. We stared at each other for a few moments. His face was unreadable. It was an expression my father would get sometimes causing my mother to joke that he was thinking too many thoughts at once.

I was desperate to know what Matthew was thinking. Maybe I was desperate enough to open the door. At the very least I was hoping to convince Matthew to keep his damn mouth shut and give me time. He owed me that much.

I grabbed my cellphone, held up my hand, walked to the back door, flipped the latch then took a few steps back.

I nodded at him, and Matthew turned the knob then slowly stepped into my kitchen. My stomach wretched at the thought of him in the place I come to escape my troubles.

"You have ten minutes." I held up my phone. "Then I'm calling the police." I closed my hand around the handle of a nearby steak knife, just in case.

"I didn't come here to hurt you." His eyes flicked to the knife.

"Again. You mean you didn't come here to hurt me again," I said deadpan.

"I deserved that."

"You deserve a lot more," I spat at him. "What do you want?"

He pointed to the fridge.

"It's his, isn't it?"

My face flushed with anger. I drew in another calming breath.

"Now you have five minutes."

"Hey, I had to ask." He raised his hands in a defenseless position.

"No, you didn't," I said through clenched teeth.

"Does he know?"

"No, and I would appreciate it if you keep this to yourself until I'm ready to tell him. It should come from me."

He didn't answer and his gaze kept drifting from the refrigerator to my face. "Listen, Callie," he said finally after clearing his throat. "Can I call you Callie?"

"No."

"Calypso, then?"

"No."

He paused surveying me. I looked at my watch and raised my eyebrows letting him know he was running out of time.

"Listen, Alex is my best friend. I've known him my whole life. We're practically brothers. I was trying to protect him."

"Wow," I chuckled. "If that's how you treat your friends, I hate to see how your enemies fare. Oh, wait…that's me." I added and glared at him. His face set and he continued.

"I came here for two reasons. One I —"

"How did you find me?" I cut him off. "The only person who knows I'm here is my father, and I doubt he'd be very forthcoming after what you did to him."

Matthew swallowed and glanced at the floor with a look that might have resembled shame on a normal human being, but I doubted the man in my kitchen was capable of such an emotion.

"I hired a private investigator." He shrugged. I huffed out

an exasperated chuckle and rolled my eyes.

"Was it the same private investigator you hired to take those pictures?"

"Look, Ca—" He was about to use my name, and he stopped himself. "*Those* pictures weren't planned. They were only supposed to be of the property. I had no fucking clue you and Alex would be..." He stopped himself from finishing that sentence and refocused. "Look, I came here for two reasons. One: I needed to find out what's so fucking special about you. What did you to do to him? I've never seen Alex like this. He's losing his edge. At first, I thought it was burn out, and maybe he needed a break. But this is something different. He's turning into someone I don't recognize since he met you."

His words should have been comforting, but it just meant that Alex enjoyed fucking me while he and Matthew were plotting to fuck me over.

"What did I *do* to him? I didn't *do* anything to him. Did it ever occur to you that there was nothing *special* about me? Did it ever occur to you that maybe Alex found something *special* about himself that he'd never realized was there? Something he'd always wanted but didn't think was possible? Something that made him truly happy for the first time in his life?" I swallowed a lump in my throat and blinked furiously, insisting that I would drop dead before I shed a tear in front of this asshole.

I was talking about myself. That was how Alex made me feel about myself every single day until the day he didn't. I couldn't speak for Alex, of course. I had no idea how he felt, and I wasn't even sure if the man I fell in love with ever existed. My words seemed to resonate with Matthew because his tone changed and he was no longer looking at me.

"I thought if I could, I don't know, break the spell, he would come to his senses and shit would go back to normal."

"And you thought showing a sixty-five year old man photos of his twenty-three year old daughter having sex in an elevator was a good solution?"

"*Sixty-five year old man?*" he scoffed, facing me again. "If you're gonna paint the picture of your father as some fragile old man who hands out peppermint candies and feeds birds in the park, I could tell you some stories that—"

"Your time is up. Get out of my house."

"I will. I need to say this one last thing." He sighed and fixed his gaze on me so firmly I unconsciously took a step back, covering my belly with the hand holding my cell phone.

"I'm... sorry," he said. I blinked a few times. This was the last thing I expected him to say. His apology was intense, awkward and seemed to be painful. He probably didn't have a lot of experience apologizing, but it didn't matter. His actions were disgusting. I would never forgive him for what he did. Ever. No matter how pitiful his attempts at contrition were.

"What I did was wrong. I know it's something I can never

undo and I don't expect you to forgive me," he continued.

Was he reading my mind?

"But I need to tell you that for whatever it's worth, Alex had no idea what I was planning. And it's fucked up because I hurt you and you didn't deserve it. I also hurt my best friend who I was trying to protect. This is completely uncharted territory for me. I don't know how to fucking fix this." He clearly wasn't talking to me anymore. He ran his fingers through his blonde hair nervously. The look on his face was sad, desperate and confused, but I couldn't garner an ounce of sympathy for him. I couldn't be sure he was even telling the truth. What if Alex sent him here to lie to me? I hated that I could no longer trust my instincts.

"Well, that's all I came to say. I'll leave now." He turned and walked to the door, turning the knob and pulling it open. Then he turned to me and I shielded my belly again. "I'm not gonna tell him." He flicked his chin towards the refrigerator.

"Thank you," I whispered then called out to him, "Hey?"

He raised his eyebrows at me.

"Do you think he'll be happy or…" I felt so stupid asking this question when I didn't trust the person giving me the answer, but I couldn't help myself. I had no one else to ask. Matthew was the person who knew Alex best.

"Honestly, I have no idea." He shrugged, and my heart sank. "But if I had to guess…this new Alex…" He nodded his head. "Yeah. He'd be pretty happy."

TWENTY EIGHT

ALEXANDER

*M*att was here earlier. It had been a few days since he'd agreed to take over and I hadn't seen him since our last conversation. He was on the island checking on some of the properties and stopped by to check on me.

We've formed a truce deciding our lifelong friendship was too precious lose over a property though I still haven't completely forgiven him for what he did to Callie.

And to me.

He was still trying for forgiveness, but Callie's absence was like a knife in the gut, and he'd put it there. Our friendship would recover, but it was going to take a long time.

I got up, padded into the kitchen to grab a beer and saw a large yellow envelope on the counter that wasn't there before. Matt's scribble was on it, and it read:

I'm sorry. I didn't know.

I used a knife to slice the top of the envelope and dumped the contents on the counter.

My heart dropped.

It was Callie's bikini bottoms and a memory card.

I know why Matt didn't hand these to me. He didn't want to get his ass kicked again. The anger started to bubble up again as I began thinking about everything the contents of this envelope had cost me.

I picked up the memory card and started to turn it over in my hand. I knew this was a bad idea, but I grabbed my laptop and inserted it into the slot anyway. Clicking through the pictures told me they were standard surveying shots: photos of the property, restaurants, pools, and beach. Then I saw a photo of the elevator and another and another.

There was a photo of two figures in the elevator and then another. Each picture was getting clearer and closer like the photographer was using a telephoto lens. Soon, I was able to make out the figures. It was me kissing Callie's lips. I was kissing Callie's chest, then her stomach. Next, I was on my knees. My head was obscured by Callie's thigh. Her face was contorted in ecstasy. The fact that these pictures existed was repulsive, but I also realized that this was the first time I'd seen Callie since she left. I didn't have one single photo or video of her. She was always the one snapping selfies.

"Memories are precious."

I would give anything for one of those pictures.

Finally, Callie's watch went off. We shared a final kiss, and she exited the elevator. The photographer went back to snapping photos of the beach, and I didn't know why, but it gave me a small measure of comfort that the photographer stumbled on us accidentally and this wasn't some premeditated scheme on Matt's part. It also explained why he was as shocked to see Callie at the meeting as I was. He probably assumed she was a random chick and he'd show me the pictures then we'd laugh about it over a couple of beers. It didn't excuse what he ended up doing with them.

I was absentmindedly clicking the arrow key until something stopped me. I clicked back a few shots, and I saw a small cottage. I didn't remember anything in any of the information about The Sterling that mentioned beach-front cottages. Something about it struck me as strange.

THE STEAM ROSE from the first shower I've taken in days. I made myself a cup of coffee and drank it out of a mug Callie bought me as a joke that read, *A little Calypso makes everything better.* The sun blinded me as I ventured outside for the first time in over a week.

The ride in the elevator was rough, but my curiosity was stronger than my self-pity, and it felt good to have a purpose. The beach was packed with guests, and I looked around seeing no sign of the cottage. I started to jog to the far side, away from the elevator, and the crowd thinned until it was deserted. I was almost at the point where the cliff sloped to meet the sand, and I saw a rocky path leading to the small house in the photo. Soft Caribbean music was wafting from the window as I approached. A stern looking woman met me. She was the woman I saw talking to Callie on the field before we met, but she was not happy to see me.

"What are you doing here?" she shouted. "Get out of here before I call the police."

"What is this place?" I asked, trying to peer around her and taking steps toward the front door causing her to back up.

"It's none of your business," she spat. "That's what it is. Haven't you caused enough trouble?" Her words suddenly made something click into place. Callie just wasn't going to swim every morning, she was coming to this house. Hope began to blossom in my chest as I started marching towards the house.

"Callie," I screamed. "Callie."

"Calypso is not in there, you fool," she hissed. "And keep your voice down."

"Tianna," a woman's voice called. "Who is that? Who's here?"

"No one, Mimi," she called back, narrowing her eyes at me. "Just a vagrant who's lost his way."

"Vagrants are my favorite kind of people," the voice called back laughing. "Tell him to come in."

Her eyes narrowed as she stepped aside shaking her head, and I ventured into the house. Bells tinkled softly as I pushed the door open. I was immediately greeted with Callie's scent, but not quite her scent it was sweeter, more floral. The cottage was small but beautifully decorated. It felt familiar and comforting. The walls were covered with photos. The assortment of quality told me the photos must have spanned decades. There were brightly colored sticky notes placed randomly around the room, and I thought I recognized Callie's handwriting on some of them. Before I could get a closer look, the voice spoke again.

"I was wondering when I would get to meet you," it said. The woman attached to the voice turned to face me, and my jaw dropped.

Suddenly everything made sense. Her face held the answer to every question I'd been asking since I set foot on this island. At one glance, I knew exactly who she was. I was staring at the second most beautiful woman I'd ever seen because the first was her daughter.

———

IT WAS like looking at a glimpse of my future with Callie with subtle differences. Her cheeks were slightly hollowed, and her eyes had laugh lines, but otherwise, she could be Callie's sister. While Callie's skin is light golden brown, her mother's skin was a deeper tone like copper. They had the same mane of long brown curly hair, but while Callie has a mixture of curls and waves, her mother's hair was darker with ringlets, but the most striking difference was in the eyes. Callie had her father's steel gray eyes, but the woman before me had eyes that were a sparkling emerald green with flecks of golden brown. I noticed that Callie also inherited her kissable nose from her mother, in opposition to her father's thin pointed nose.

The first mystery she solved is why The Closer gave up everything and disappeared. One look and I was ready to do the same thing for Callie. It also explained Callie's mysterious beach trips every morning. But it raised more questions.

She held her hands out to me, and she was swaying her hips to the music.

"Dance with me," she commanded, and I immediately obliged wondering if any man could deny a request from this woman. "Tianna, dear, make me a video of this. I don't want to forget it." The other woman pulled out a smartphone and began recording. "You know," she continued, pulling me closer, "my mother always used to say that you can tell a lot…"

"…about a man by the way he dances." I thought to myself as she continued out loud, "and I can tell that you have a good heart and that you love my daughter very much." My chest constricted and tears stung my eyes. I blinked them away.

"I do. I love her so much. I love her more than anything else in the world."

A brilliant smile lit up her face, and she pulled away from me.

She reached for a tablet and held it out to me. The screen was filled with a selfie of Callie and me at Bathsheba Beach. I swiped left and saw us at The Animal Flower Cave. I kept swiping and saw the photographic evidence of the happiest times in my life. I couldn't stop the tears, and my face was burning with shame, but I couldn't help it. She took the tablet and grabbed me by the hand pulling me towards the door of the cottage.

"Take me to the sea." Another command. We waded into the water and sat letting the waves wash over us. She took my large hand into her two small ones and placed them in her lap. "Let me tell you a story…" she began.

TWENTY NINE

ALEXANDER

I was sprinting towards the elevator and regretting skipping the gym for weeks. In the elevator, I caught my breath, but when the doors opened, I took off again. I ran past the private suites, the villas, the main building and now I was barreling top speed down the path to Callie's house with my legs and arms pumping in opposition. After running down the path, I leaped up the patio steps and pounded on the door.

"Callie," I screamed at the top of my lungs. "I get it. I understand—" The door swung open and I was face to face with The Closer.

"I thought I told you never to come back here." His eyes narrowed. "And besides you're too late. Calypso is back at school." He tried to slam the door. I put my foot between the door and the jamb preventing him from closing it.

"I met Amelia," I said, still panting. I was *really* out of shape. "I met Amelia. I know why you won't sell."

His face softened slightly, but he was still pissed. He opened the door a few more inches.

"Well." He looked at me. "If you met my wife, then you know why I *can't* sell." He rolled his eyes and huffed. "You might as well come in." He opened the door even wider, stepped aside to let me in, and I saw Matt sitting on his couch. He jumped up when he saw me and walked toward the door. He shook hands with Barnabas Sterling, gave him a nod and looked at me.

"Matt, what are you doing here?" I asked. He patted my shoulder and squeezed past me.

"We'll talk later, bro," he called over his shoulder as I watched him walk up the path.

"So, you've been dying to get into this house for weeks," The Closer called to me. "Are you planning to stay on the patio all day once you've finally been invited in?"

HE HANDED ME A TOWEL, and I dried off as best I could before taking a seat on the couch. The house was expertly decorated. It reminded me of the cottage and my private suite. Then I guessed that they must have all been decorated by the same person, Amelia. There were photos of The Sterlings at various ages and another woman I didn't recognize but looked almost exactly like Callie.

"Jennifer," Mr. Sterling called out, answering my question. "Amelia's younger sister. We lost her about a year ago. Breast Cancer."

236 | CHERISHING THE GODDESS

I nodded.

"What's your drink?" He indicated a shelf of glass bottles and decanters.

"Scotch," I replied. "But I'm becoming partial to rum."

"Yeah, I'll bet you are." He gave me a mirthless chuckle and handed me a glass.

"Do you know why we named our daughter, Calypso?"

I shook my head.

"Have you ever read The Odyssey?"

"I pretended to in prep school," I said. He gave me a look that told me Callie must have gotten her sense of humor from her mother.

"Calypso was a goddess. When Odysseus lands on her island paradise, she enchants him and keeps him captive until she is commanded to release him by Zeus so he can return to his wife, Penelope."

I saw exactly where he was going with this story.

"A little over twenty-five years ago I landed on this island with a bunch of my mates for Crop-Over."

I shrugged and shook my head. He laughed.

"It's an island-wide party. Food. Dancing. Drinking. Music. And the women," he grinned wistfully, and I was feeling a little uncomfortable. "The finale is called Grand Kadooment. It's a huge parade party. My mates and I were standing on the side watching the parade go past when this gorgeous woman in the tiniest costume wearing a big feather headdress and wings pulled me into a dance.

"I don't know why she chose me. I've wondered every day since. She had the most captivating smile and these big, dazzling green eyes. I felt like I was hypnotized. Do you know what I mean?"

I smiled. I knew exactly what he meant.

"Then she was gone. She let go of my hand, rejoined the parade and disappeared.

"I searched for her the rest of day, and finally after two more days of searching, I found her again. Her father owned a restaurant in St. Michael and she would wait tables. I sat a table for lunch every day for a week, chatting her up until she agreed to a proper date. I never left her again." He was smiling at the memory, and I was thinking of mine and Callie's negotiation in the office and of course, our daily second-breakfast dates.

"You see, my Penelope was the boardroom. She was a cold-hearted bitch, and I didn't miss her at all. Sure, we had some good times, but she didn't compare to I found with Amelia. One day with that woman's smile and I knew I done with everything else.

"So I'm asking you, Alexander Wolfe. What do you have to go back to?"

He was asking me, point-blank, the question Callie was trying to ask me in the shower, and I shrugged it off then. In the back of my mind, I figured I was smart enough to find a way to have it all, but the thought of my work schedule and it taking me away from Callie made me sick. I didn't want to face it then, but now with Callie gone, it was obvious.

"Nothing, sir." I met his eyes. "Without Callie, I have nothing."

"I thought you might say that." He sighed and refilled my drink.

"You know, my wife's father hated me."

I did know this, but I didn't let on.

"I was too rich, too British, too educated. Didn't think I was good enough for his little girl. He was right. Amelia was way too good for a berk like me, but I didn't care. I loved her. I would do anything for her. I even bought her this resort. It was always her dream to own her own hotel. So I made sure she had the biggest and the best. It was also worth to see the look on the old bastard's face when I delivered the deed to Amelia." He took another sip of his drink. I huffed out a chuckle, and he gave me a half smile. "You know the owner of this place wasn't eager to sell it to me at first. It took a little," he paused swirling the liquid in his glass, "convincing."

Our eyes met. A laugh I tried to suppress escaped my chest and echoed around the living room. After a second, The Closer joined me, and we were both laughing hysterically. There was nothing funny. It was a sort of maniacal, knee-jerk reaction to the absurdity of our situation. He didn't deserve to be with Amelia any more than I deserved to be with Callie, but here we were, two demons who by dumb luck or fate managed to find two angels that didn't make us feel like the monsters we were. We were hopelessly in love and there was nothing we could do about it.

"Bloody fucking irony." He finally chuckled, and his face grew serious.

"A few years ago, Amelia started to get a little forgetful. We didn't think much of it. She'd misplace her keys, have trouble finding a word or think she didn't do something when she had." He polished off his rum and refilled it.

"One day, I get a call from the police. Amelia had been trying to take a little girl from a department store in Bridgetown. She kept calling her Calypso. The little girl was four. Calypso was sixteen at the time." He was holding the glass, staring off into space.

"She was diagnosed with early-onset Alzheimer's disease. That was seven years ago. She was only forty-six. The youngest case her doctor had ever heard of." He gulped again and placed the glass on the counter behind him. "We've explored every treatment option available. I've threatened, bribed and bullied her way into every drug trial. We've flown to every cognitive specialist in the world, flown some here. The therapies, treatments, and medications help. The doctors say it's a miracle she's remained as sharp as she has for this long. She thinks is due to prayer and bathing in the ocean every day."

"And you?" I asked. He huffed out another mirthless chuckle.

"I think it's the millions of dollars I've spent on experimental treatments and medications, but what the hell do I know? We're delaying the inevitable. There's still no cure. Everybody's close when your checkbook is out. Mimi would always tell me that I couldn't open my wallet to solve every problem and *this* was how she decided to prove her point. That stubborn wife of mine." He smirked and shook his head.

"She has more good days than bad days but the bad days are awful. She always remembers me, but sometimes she can't believe how old I am," he chuckled. "She usually remembers Calypso, but more and more she thinks she's Jennifer."

I look at him, and he senses my question.

"She knows Jennifer's gone most days. Occasionally, I have to tell her, and that's not easy."

"The cottage?" I asked.

"The cottage is the home she and Jennifer grew up in, in St. Michael. Every once in a while she'd get disoriented in the house, and the doctors thought it would help to have more familiar surroundings. I had it brought over brick by brick and put it on the beach. Jennifer oversaw the project, to make sure it was perfect and would even stay there with Amelia from time to time."

"Who's the woman with her?"

"That's Tianna. She was the nurse that helped deliver Calypso. She had lost her husband and was left with four young children. She and Amelia became fast friends, and Amelia insisted we hire her at The Sterling. We paid her a nurse's salary, and Amelia suggested she bring her children to work so she wouldn't have to pay for childcare. She worked her way up to head of housekeeping and maintenance. She put all four kids through college. Two of them work here. They're like cousins to our daughter.

"I could tell you dozens of stories like that about my wife. She's the heart and soul of this place. So, when Amelia needed full-time care, Tianna didn't hesitate. She didn't want a stranger caring for her, and she won't take a penny for it either."

I sat in silence for a long time, turning my glass around in my hand.

"Son." He put his hand on my shoulder. "I'm telling you all this because Amelia's Alzheimer's is hereditary. There's a blood test Calypso could take to find out if she carries the gene, but she refused. She said if she was positive she would want to spend her life building memories, not waiting to lose them, but if her mother has it, then it's possible…"

I looked at him like he was crazy.

"Sir." I stood and faced him, and I couldn't believe what he was suggesting. "If you knew then about Amelia what you know now—"

"I'd wish I'd met her sooner so I could have more time and cherish every moment."

"Then, I need your help."

THIRTY

CALYPSO

*T*oday was one of those September days that felt like summer. I still couldn't believe it had been over a month since I'd left Barbados and I'd been living at the beach house for three weeks. It felt like a lifetime.

I finally decided to withdraw from all of my classes, but early enough that it wouldn't affect my standing when I decided to return—if I decided to return.

My parents and I video chatted every day and they were very understanding. Mum wished I would come back to Barbados, and I planned to, but I still wasn't ready.

I'd just spent a few hours at the beach sunbathing, and I was walking back to the house to start making myself dinner and dig into the pile of books I picked up from the library in town.

Something felt off when I put the key in the lock and entered the foyer. With a hand placed instinctively over my belly, I grabbed an umbrella from the stand, tip-toeing carefully forward holding the umbrella by the tip, so if there was an intruder, I would nail them with the wooden handle.

"Who's there?" I called out and rolled my eyes at my stupidity. Was I expecting someone to call out "*a burglar?*" To my surprise, a familiar voice called to me from two feet away.

"Callie," he said. I screamed and jumped, dropping the umbrella and clawing for the light switch. I found it, flipped it up, and there he was, Alexander Wolfe, illuminated in my foyer.

"Alex. What the fuck are you doing here?" I started hitting him in his arms and chest, more as punishment for scaring me than any of the other reasons I was mad at him. "You scared the shit out of me. How did you get in my house?"

"I didn't mean to scare you." He was gripping my wrists to stop the onslaught of slaps, and it reminded me of the last time we were together. Alex sensed it too and quickly released my hands. "I needed to see you."

"So you break into my house?" I was taking deep breaths trying to get my heart rate under control. "How did you find me?"

"Your dad told me where to find you," he said. This shocked me, but it still left questions.

"My dad doesn't have a key," I said. "So again, did you break into my house?"

"Well, technically," he started, and he was wearing a

sheepish smile that I still found very sexy in spite of myself. "I didn't break in, and it's not your house."

"What?"

"I bought the house," he blurted out.

Un-fucking-believable.

"So, now I have to move." I crossed my arms and glared at him.

"To be honest, buying the house to get you to talk me seemed a lot more romantic when I was doing it but now when I see your face, it seems it might not have been the best idea..."

"You think?" I tilted my head and raised my eyebrows. He was making the most adorably pitiful face, and I felt my resolve slipping. I took a deep breath and turned to walk up the stairs.

"Where are you going?" he called as I turned my back on him.

"To pack."

"Callie, could you please talk to me, let me explain?"

"No."

"Hear me out, and I promise I'll leave you alone forever."

I snorted laughter.

"You need a better line, Mr. Wolfe. That one's getting tired."

"Okay, wait. I'll be right back. Don't move." He turned and left.

I paused at the bottom of the stairs as I heard the front door click. In an instant, there was a knock on the door. Alex was on the other side of the door, grinning at me and pointing at the knob. It took everything I had not to laugh.

"It's open," I called to him, rolling my eyes as he opened the door and came back in. He was holding a large manila envelope and a big white box with a red bow.

"First things, first." He dumped the contents of the envelope onto the foyer table, scribbled something on one of the pages and slid it over to me. "There. Now you are the official owner of this house, and I am your guest."

"Thank you." I uncrossed my arms. "Now get out."

"I have another gift for you." He took a step towards me holding the box out. He was wearing my favorite grin, and I saw his dimples were just where I left them.

"I don't want it." I shrugged, though I was curious. He took a step closer and shook the box. A familiar smell wafted into the room. I looked at him suspiciously. He grinned his smug grin, and I was once again the canary in this scenario.

The box was surprisingly warm when I snatched it from his hands. I placed it on the table, ripped the ribbon off and removed the lid. The smell grew stronger, and my stomach growled in anticipation. Alex heard it and chuckled. Inside the box was another zippered quilted box. I unzipped it and inside were two paper bags. I ripped them open and jackpot: flying fish and they were still hot and steamy. I looked at Alex in disbelief.

"Claudette says hi." He was incredibly smug. "And she thinks you should hear me out."

I shoved an entire piece in my mouth and closed my eyes, savoring every bite.

"You have five minutes," I said through a mouthful of fish.

"Ten?" he countered, and I glared at him.

"Okay." He smiled. "Five."

WE WALKED over the couch in the sitting room, and Alex proceeded to explain everything. He told me about Matt, the photos and how Matt got his hands on my bikini bottoms; how he only came to Barbados to meet my dad that our rendezvous in the elevator was a lucky coincidence. I found out how he got those bruises on his face and that my parents still owned The Sterling. He also told me that Matt apologized to my father in person and hand delivered the contracts revoking the sale. He quickly added that Matthew was ready to apologize to me and I wished I could've seen the look on his face when Alex punched him, but I knew Matthew had at least told me the truth. He really did find me to apologize and Alex was really blameless. I was also secretly grateful that he kept his promise to keep our meeting a secret and was hoping he was right about the last thing he told me.

As he continued to speak, our bodies were moving closer and closer together. By the time he told me about meeting my mother and his conversation with my dad, I was wrapped in his arms, and his chin was resting on the top of my head. I knew then that my heart knew the truth all along, but my mind needed more time to catch up. My mother's words echoed, "*My heart recognizes you. Does that make sense?*" Somewhere deep down inside I knew Alex was always mine.

"I'm sorry I didn't believe you," I whispered into his chest.

"Not as sorry as I am." He kissed the top of my head again. "That was the longest month of my life."

"I told you that I trusted you and at the first opportunity to test that trust I—"

"Callie, I understand." He squeezed me a little tighter and kissed my head again. "You never should have been put in that position, but I meant it when I said you owned my heart. I promise you will never have a reason to doubt me again." He slid his finger down the bridge of my nose before tilting my chin up to kiss me.

"I'm glad you met my mother. I've been telling her about you for weeks," I said when our lips parted and I snuggled into his chest again.

"I know. And you sent *her* pictures." He tickled me and I giggled.

"I really wanted to tell you about her, and I know you were curious about where I was going every morning."

"Gorgeous, curious is putting it mildly, but I get it. You

were trying to protect her from the big bad wolf who was coming to huff and puff and blow her house down." He laughed.

"That analogy was too perfect. How long have you been working on that one?" I smirked.

"It was a five-hour flight, and I had to do something to keep me from eating the fish. The interior of my plane smells like Oistin's."

"Mmmm." I reached for a piece and fed it to Alex before helping myself to another.

"So was *going to the beach* a code name for my benefit?"

"No. It was really hard for my dad when my mum started living in the cottage full time. So, we started calling it *going to the beach* and we've never stopped."

Alex planted a kiss on the top of my head. "Your mom is pretty amazing."

"I know." I sighed.

"You're lucky I didn't meet her first." He tickled me again.

"Um, first of all. Gross!" I slapped him in the chest, and Alex chuckled. "And second of all, *you're* lucky you didn't meet my mum first. My dad would have actually killed you. He loves me, but my mum... He adores her. I've never seen anything like it." I pushed myself off of his chest and cradled his cheeks in my palms. "Until I met you."

He pulled me close and kissed me for a long time. If kisses

had words, Alex's would say, *"I love you. I miss you. I need you."*

"So, all this happened, yesterday?" I asked when I separated our lips so I could catch my breath.

"Yup," he replied.

"Wow," I sighed.

"Wow," he agreed.

"So what do we do now?" I asked. He grinned and raised his eyebrow. I laughed. "That's not exactly what I meant," though I would be lying if the thought hadn't been crossing my mind after I got over the initial shock of seeing Alex in my foyer. "When do you go back to work?"

"I don't," he replied as if I'd asked him what time it was. I furrowed my brow in confusion. "I gave the company to Matt. Well, I promoted Matt to CEO. I still have the majority stake. I have a feeling I'll be spending a lot of money on flying fish." He kissed my temple after I elbowed him in the ribs. "I should have been honest with myself sooner about the way I felt about you. I never imagined myself feeling like this about anyone. I was raised to believe that people come and go, but the company was forever. Then I met you. I was smart enough to know I never wanted to let you go, but I was stupid to think I could hold on to everything else at the same time. You are my everything else, Callie. Companies come and go, but the people you love are forever."

"So what does that mean, Alexander Wolfe?"

He leaned forward and slid off of the couch and on to one knee. He was holding up a ring.

A very familiar ring.

"Where did you get this?"

"Where do you think?"

Tears pricked the back of my eyes as I felt him slide the ring on my finger. I grabbed the sides of his face and kissed him. He wrapped one arm around my waist and pulled me into him. I felt him slide the other arm under my knees and he lifted me.

"Was that a yes?" he whispered. His lips lightly brushed mine as he spoke.

"Take me upstairs, and I'll show you," I whispered.

"Man, you Sterling women are bossy."

THIRTY ONE

CALYPSO

*U*pstairs, Alex kicked open the bedroom door, and set me down on the bed before kicking off his shoes, pulling off his shirt, and crawling onto the mattress. He grabbed the hem of my tank top and pulled it off. I was still wearing my bikini. He eyed me quizzically.

"You look different…"

I felt my face flush.

"I put on a few pounds." I smiled sheepishly. "And it looks like I'm not the only one." I poked his middle. He was still in amazing shape but not as chiseled.

"I missed a couple of workouts," he shrugged and smiled, "but this…" He ran a hand over my plusher middle. "I love it." He grabbed handfuls of my breasts through my bikini top. "Especially these. These are definitely bigger."

"And sore." I winced, tenderly pushing his hands away.

"Come here, Goddess. I'll be gentle."

He kissed me and began to taste my body, planting little kisses, nibbles and licks everywhere he could reach. He pulled the strings on my bikini top, releasing my breasts before covering them with his mouth and gently licking and sucking on each nipple. He moved down my belly, moaning his approval at my new softer physique as he licked and sucked his way down to the wetness between my thighs.

Feeling him worship me like this was better than I ever remembered and I felt myself beginning to spasm as he removed my bottoms, and began to part my legs.

"Not yet, goddess," he whispered. "Hold on a little longer."

I didn't know if I could. It had been too long, and my body craved his touch more than I'd realized. When I finally felt his mouth close over my center, I exploded into him. I screamed his name as I buried my fingers in his dark hair. He tasted me through my ecstasy, and it felt so amazing, familiar, and beautiful.

"God, I've missed you," he moaned into my thighs as the waves of my climax subsided. He quickly kicked out of his pants, grabbed me by the waist and rolled me on top of him. "I want to see you. I want to see everything."

I guided the tip of his cock into me as I slowly lowered myself, feeling him deliciously stretching me as my body devoured his full length. He placed his hands on my hips and guided me up and down as I rocked my hips back and forth. Our pace started to quicken and Alex reached between my legs and rubbed rub my clit in a circular motion. I gasped and moaned.

"Look at me," he whispered. I looked down at Alex and found his ocean blue eyes devouring me as if he were trying to commit every contour of my face to memory. I leaned forward, and our lips met. "Don't you ever leave me again."

"Not a chance," I whispered.

I felt Alex's body clench under mine, and I followed with my own release. We rocked together riding the wave of our climaxes, and I wondered how I ever thought I could have lived without this. I slid off of him, and into my favorite spot in the crook of his arm.

"Alex, are you sure?" I whispered. He looked at me confused. "About giving up your company for me."

"Yes." He took my chin in his thumb and forefinger, and kissed me. "I'm doing it for me." He smirked. "My company made me rich, you make me happy."

"And you're happy?" I asked.

"Nothing could make me happier than spending the rest of my life with you in my arms." He relaxed and squeezed me closer to him before climbing out bed, and walking into the bathroom.

I hoped he was wrong.

"Babe, could you go get me a bottle of water from the fridge downstairs? I'm thirsty."

"I live to serve you," he answered in a deep silly voice. He kissed me, took two steps towards the door then ran back to the bed and kissed me again. "You're not going to be asleep when I get back up here, are you?" he teased.

"Go." I laughed as he kissed me a third time, and I reclined onto the pillows and waited.

———

"CALLIE?" he called from downstairs a few seconds later. "What is this?"

A smile crept across my face. "What is what, babe?" I called back in feigned ignorance. "You have to be more specific. There's a lot of stuff down there."

Moments later, I heard him bounding up the stairs.

"This." He was waving the piece of paper the doctor gave me at my last visit. I'd never moved it. "This. Is this what I think it is?" He filled the doorway with his chest heaving from the effort of tearing through the house while wearing an excited, hopeful expression. I grinned, secretly relieved to see how happy he was.

"Where's my water?" I laughed.

He narrowed his eyes and waved the sonogram again.

"If you think it's our baby's first photo." I tucked my bottom lip between my teeth. "Then..." I shrugged.

He screamed and jumped on the bed, kissing me everywhere. Then he paused with his face over my belly. He kissed my navel.

"Hi, baby," he whispered. "I'm your dad." Then he looked up at me, and I saw his blue eyes were sparkling with tears. "Oh, Callie." He sighed and kissed me. "How?"

"Well, when a man and a woman really love each other—" I started to giggle when Alex growled and began peppering my neck with kisses. "My doctor says it happens sometimes with the pill, even when you take it religiously. So, this is okay? You're happy about this?"

Kissing a trail up my belly, over my chest, across my throat before landing on my lips was how he answered my question.

"Are you happy about this?" He leaned up to look into my eyes and with one hand stroked my cheek. I let out a deep sigh.

"I did consider all of my options, options that I've been grateful for in the past," I paused to gauge his reaction to my words. His face was impassive. There was no judgment. I exhaled. "I mean, with Mum, school, and… us." His thumb brushed over my cheek. "I wasn't sure I could handle it all, but I decided that I was ready to do this, whatever that means." I gave him a small smile and he leaned forward and pressed his lips to mine.

"When did you find out?"

"A week after I got back to school."

He nodded solemnly with an expression that might have been guilt.

"I was going to tell you. I planned to move back home in a few weeks and I thought it would be easier to handle with my family around me, just in case…" My voice trailed off and I swallowed a lump that had formed in my throat.

"Callie, your dad told me about a genetic test…" He trailed off.

My father didn't waste any time. He'd gone from hating Alex one minute to recruiting him to carry on his seven-year crusade to get me to do the genetic screening in the next.

"I'm negative."

He sat up and looked at me. "Your father said you refused to get tested."

"I did, until I found out I was pregnant. I was still unsure about everything…with us and I wanted to be prepared. My doctor advised against it. She said the stress might be too much to handle if either of the tests were positive, but I insisted. I was tested for the breast cancer gene, too. Also negative. It's not a guarantee, but it's hope."

Alex exhaled, pulled me closer to him and kissed my temple. "I'm so sorry you went through that alone."

I wrapped my arms around him and squeezed.

"So, what are you going to do about Wharton?"

"School?" I replied with a smirk.

"Yeah." He laughed. "School."

"Well, I definitely want to finish. So, I guess I'll have to figure that out."

"*We* will have to figure that out," he corrected me.

"Together. And if you want to finish school, then that's what's gonna happen."

I leaned up and kissed him.

"And after?" he asked.

"Well," I reached up and stroked his face, "I've been giving that a lot of thought, too. I've decided that I want to go home and stay there." I paused trying to read his face for a reaction to my words. It was again expressionless. "I'd always dreamed of having a life like the one Dad had before he met my mum and now that I've had a taste of it. I don't think it's for me," I continued. Alex opened his mouth to protest and I placed my fingers over his lips. "I'm not saying that I'm not cut out for it or that I couldn't handle it. I'm just saying that I don't want to. I want to spend as much time with Mum as I can and Dad is going to need help running The Sterling soon. Plus, I love Barbados. It's my home and I can't imagine living anywhere else. Would you be okay with that? I mean, I guess we could split our time between New York and Barbados if—"

"The only thing I had left in New York was Wolfe and my home is wherever you are. I told you before, I want to stay this close to you for as long as you'll let me. Would you be okay with that?"

"I would be very okay with that." I reached up, wrapped my arms around his neck and pulled him down for a kiss. As our mouths connected and our tongues began to tangle and caress each other, Alex propped himself up on his elbows careful not press the full weight of his body on mine. I pulled away and gazed into the irises that were my favorite color and so full of love for me, and our baby. "I love you, Alexander Wolfe."

"I love you too, Calypso Sterling."

He lay down beside me, and I took my place in the crook of his arm. He put one of his hands on my belly, splaying his fingers while holding the sonogram over our heads with the other, examining it carefully.

"Okay." He kissed my forehead. "So, what am I looking at here?"

"This little black bubble is the amniotic sac," I pointed, "and this little thing inside that looks like a wad of chewing gum is our baby."

He clutched the print out to his chest scandalized. "Don't talk about my baby that way," he gasped and I giggled before rolling over to kiss him.

I held up the pearl ring to admire it. "My preciousss," I hissed.

"You're not going to bite off my finger and start eating raw fish, are you?" He laughed and reached out to tickle me before stopping himself, making me giggle at his overly cautious behavior. Matthew was right. This new Alex was *pretty happy* about becoming a father.

"I don't know." I shrugged. "I've heard pregnancy cravings can get pretty weird."

Alex let out one of his surprise belly laughs that I missed every single day for last month.

"So my mother just gave this to you?" I asked. He took my hand, and now we were both gazing at the ring.

"She said I earned it, and that you would tell me what that means." He turned to me with a raised eyebrow. I laughed and turned to face him.

"This ring—" I wiggled my finger. "—was my grandmother's. My grandfather was in the US Navy. I'm not sure if he was stationed in Barbados or on shore leave, but he met my grandmother somehow, and fell head over heels in love with her, but she wanted nothing to do with him."

"This sounds like déjà vu." He was smoothing his palm over my belly.

"Hush, you." I kissed him again. "So, she didn't want to go out with him because Navy men had a reputation of showing up, romancing the local women, and disappearing. Not her style. But, he kept telling her he was different and wanted an opportunity to prove himself."

"Okay, this sounds really familiar." He laughed. I narrowed my eyes at him. "All right, I'm listening."

"So, she asked him to get her a pearl. He tells her fine, no problem, he would buy her a pearl. No, she says, she wants him to *dive* for one and get it himself. She most likely thought that he would refuse and she would finally be rid of him, but—"

"He did it," he finished my sentence knowingly.

"He *did* it," I agree. "And nearly died in the process. He was in a coma for two days, and this was in the sixties, so they weren't sure if he was going to make it. My grandmother felt so bad that she never left his bedside. When he finally woke up and saw my grandmother's face, he said—" I had to stop for a moment because I was laughing so hard. *"Do you believe me now?!"*

Alex joined me in laughter.

"Whenever he told that story, he would always end with, *'and she's never stopped trying to kill me.'* They put the pearl in a ring, got married and lived happily ever after."

"Whoa." He was shaking his head in disbelief.

"What's wrong?" I asked.

"Nothing." He was still gazing at the sonogram, "I'm hoping this kid is a boy. The women in your family are trouble— worth it —but trouble."

THE END

EPILOGUE

ALEXANDER

"*Jenny*," I sang to the adorable freckled face girl trying to sneak past me, "*what are you do-ing?*"

"*Noth-ing,*" she sang back and flashed me the miniature version of her mother's thousand watt smile, minus a front tooth.

"*It doesn't look like noth-ing.*" I crossed to where she stood over her. She was doing her best to look innocent. I peered behind her back, then looked her in the face, and raised an eyebrow. She sighed and presented the stick she was attempting hide.

"Jenny." I laughed and had a sudden flashback of her mother attempting to fend me off with a keyboard. "What are you planning to do with that?"

"Daddy," she sighed in exasperation, dropping the act. "This boy keeps bothering me, and I asked him to stop bothering me, and I even said please, and he still didn't stop, and I told him I was gonna knock him in the head

with a stick if he didn't leave me alone and he's still bothering me, so I'm gonna hit him with this stick," she said all
in one breath, then held out the small branch.

"Okay, sounds good." I nodded. "Off you go."

"Jennifer Amelia Wolfe!" My wife's voice boomed from the
doorway of the cottage. She marched past me down the
stone path balancing our eighteen-month old, Claudia, on
her hip and making a beeline for our seven-year-old with
her other hand extended. "You will not hit that boy with a
stick. Give it here."

Her tiny face fell, and she handed over the stick reluc-
tantly. I caught her eye behind her mother's back, made a
mean face, held up my fists in a fighting stance, and
nodded my head. She mimicked me, held up her little fists
and returned my nod before running back to the beach to
join the other children playing.

"I saw that." My wife rounded on me and raised an
eyebrow. I reached out and tickled Claudia under her
chin. "Really, Alex?"

"What?" I shrugged. "She said please."

She kissed me, shook her head and strolled towards the
beach. "Maybe I should've had a stick in the elevator." She
glanced over her shoulder to the far side of the cliff at the
place where we met almost twenty-five years ago. That
old elevator had long been replaced, but we gave it a nice
send-off.

"That wouldn't have worked." I slid my arm around her
hip and squeezed, kissing her forehead. "And if memory

serves me correctly, I think I was the one that needed a stick."

She burst out laughing, making Claudia laugh, and then I joined in.

"Are you ready for this?" she asked through a wistful sigh, looking up at me.

"No," I replied sullenly. "She's too young."

"She's three months older than I was when we met." She smiled.

"That's different," I said, glancing at the elevator. She rolled her eyes.

"He's a nice boy," she reminded me.

"But his dad's an asshole."

"I won't disagree with you there." She laughed. "But he's also your best friend."

Callie claimed to have forgiven Matt years ago, but I wasn't not so sure. This woman could hold a grudge.

We saw Matt and his wife, Vittoria, strolling toward us. Callie's face broke into a wide grin, and she and Vittoria quickened their steps to meet. Vittoria took Claudia from her arms and began bouncing her up and down making kissing faces. The women immediately started to chatter in rapid Italian. Callie severely misrepresented her grasp on the language. She was fluent, but also speaks Spanish, French and could order beer and sausages in German. She was still a mystery after all these years.

Matt met Vittoria six months after I met Callie, on a business trip in Italy and fell hard. She was beautiful and incredibly smart, which must have been why she and Callie got along so well. It also helped that she took Callie's side when she found out what Matt did. She almost called off their wedding until Callie intervened on Matt's behalf.

"That woman is Matthew's only redeeming quality," she said when I questioned her motives before adding, "and he looks so pitiful on our couch."

They had a son, Matteo Alessandro and a daughter, Kimberly Vittoria.

I was hoping to have a son to name after Matt, but I think Callie kept having girls out of spite. Our first, Grace Amelia, named after my mother, was born almost nine months to the day after I met Callie. She was followed by Alexandra Amelia, Jennifer Amelia and our surprise baby, Claudia Amelia, named for her great-grandmother, whose pearl ring my wife still wears. They were all girls. Each one of them beautiful with my blue eyes, and their mother's everything else.

"Hey, old man," Matt shouted and clapped my back. "You ready to make this official?"

"I still can't believe it," I shook my head. "But I couldn't have picked a better a man for my little girl."

"Aww, you're not gonna cry again are you?" he teased.

"Like I did right after I broke your nose?" I retorted, and he laughed.

"And you deserved it, *mio pazzo*," Vittoria grabbed his cheeks with her free hand and kissed him. He absent-mindedly rubbed the bridge of his nose. There was no trace of our fist fight like there was no trace of the other fight. He made things right, and we were all good.

Just a little disagreement between brothers.

THE CEREMONY WAS intimate and beautiful. Grace was luminous, and Matteo looked like he'd won the lottery.

The reception went on well into the night, and I spent most of it holding my wife in my arms and dancing, remembering our own wedding day.

WE'D SAILED BACK to Barbados a week after I found her in Jersey. I surprised Callie with a luxury catamaran I'd christened CALYPSO that just happened to be twenty feet longer than the NADINE. It was a backup plan in case the flying fish didn't work. We spent the next two weeks sailing to Barbados and making love in every spot on the ship.

We also held on to the beach house. It came in handy when the three of us moved to Philly so Callie could finish school. Gracie also used it frequently when she decided to break my heart and attend Wharton for under-grad instead of Harvard.

Callie and I wanted to get married right away, so she

bought a dress, we got a marriage license, and waited for Tianna to give us the signal.

Three days later we got the call. Amelia was having a good day, and was excited to see her only child get married. We met on the beach in front of the cottage for a ceremony that was only supposed to be attended by Barnabas, Amelia, Matt, Tianna, Callie and myself. When word got out about the wedding, we were joined by most of the staff of The Sterling and some of the long-term guests. Even Paul and Nadine showed up in time for the reception with Claudette in tow. I placed a last minute order for my pregnant bride's favorite food.

TONIGHT, we stood on the deck of the CALYPSO, hugging and kissing our little Gracie, who wasn't little anymore. Alexandra took Jenny and Claudia back up the cliff to put them to bed. The kids were planning to sail around the Caribbean for their honeymoon before flying back to New York where she'd finish her last year of law school at Columbia, and he'd go back to work at Wolfe Industries.

"Not a scratch on this boat, Matteo," I said, squeezing his shoulders. "She's old so take it easy."

"Sure thing, Uncle Alex." He grinned and looked over at Gracie. "Or should I call you Dad?"

"No," I deadpanned. "You shouldn't."

"Don't pay attention to him." My wife slapped me on the chest and I grinned. The six of us took turns hugging again, and soon the boat was pulling away from the pier. Callie and Vittoria held hands and sobbed quietly. Matt wiped away a tear and I smirked. I caught his eye and silently mouthed the word *pussy*. He flipped me off smiling.

Callie and I said goodnight to the elder Widnickis after the younger Widnickis disappeared over the horizon. We tip-toed into the house Callie once shared with her parents that we now shared with our children. We flopped onto the couch, and she swung her feet into my lap so I could remove her shoes and massage away the soreness. She leaned her head back and closed her eyes.

My wife was as beautiful as she was the day I met her. Her long dark chestnut curls now had gray highlights, and she had these gorgeous crinkles that formed on the sides of her eyes whenever she smiled, which I tried to make her do as often as possible.

Amelia took a turn for the worse five years after we got married. Barnabas gave The Sterling to Callie and me to run before he moved into the cottage full-time to be with his wife. She held on to meet Alexandra and slipped away peacefully in her sleep. Barnabas joined her three months later.

Callie visited a specialist every year for a full battery of tests. There were still no signs of the diseases that took her mother or her aunt, but my heart stopped every time she misplaced her keys or snapped her fingers searching for a word she'd temporarily forgotten. I'd also become quite proficient at performing breast exams over the years.

There wasn't a moment that I regretted giving up everything to spend my life with her. She felt my eyes on her and turned to face me. She smiled, and I raised one eyebrow.

"Take me upstairs," she whispered.

"So bossy," I growled as I scooped her into my arms and took the steps two at a time.

WE TIPTOED PAST THE GIRLS' rooms, making out like teenagers while trying to be as quiet as possible. I tossed her on to the bed and flopped down beside her.

"God, I'm still crazy about you, Calypso." I gazed into her eyes and kissed her before unzipping her dress and pulling it over her head. She was unbuttoning my dress shirt. My lips brushed against hers before I began trailing kisses down her neck, her collarbone, and chest. The clasp of her bra unsnapped under my well-practiced hand.

Her breasts had grown larger and softer from years of breastfeeding, and I grabbed handfuls of them licking, kissing and sucking everywhere. She moaned in response to my kisses as I made my way down her body, burying my face in the softness of her belly, tracing my tongue along the uneven lines that striped her stomach and hips that deepened every time her womb blossomed. I lightly traced my fingers along her thighs, planting kisses on every dimple until I reached her knees and slowly separated them. She moaned my name, and I knew she was anxious for relief.

"Hold on, goddess," I whispered into her quivering thighs. "I'm almost there."

I'd spent almost a quarter of a century memorizing every square inch of her body, learning every curve and delicious fold. My fingers glided over her, exploring and discovering new ways to pleasure her. My lips trailed kisses on the inside of her thighs leading to the wetness between. I finally slid one of her thighs over my shoulder and lowered my face between them. I trailed my tongue through her lips until I reached her clitoris and began to suck lightly. She inhaled sharply and started to spasm. Her pussy was as sweet and delicious at forty-six as it was at twenty-three and all of the years in-between. Her fingers flew to my hair grabbing handfuls and pressing me into her, moaning in ecstasy. Once she released every drop of her nectar, I made my way back up her body until I was gazing into her hypnotizing gray eyes.

"Mrs. Wolfe," I said, kissing her.

"Yes, Mr. Underhill," she replied flashing her gorgeous grin.

"I need to be inside you," I said, waggling my eyebrows. She giggled, and she was twenty-three again.

"Do you?" She grinned.

"So, if you don't have any appointments or..."

And as if on cue, we heard a soft cry. Our faces turned to the hologram on the nightstand displaying the view of the night vision camera over Claudia's crib. We stared intently at the image, and I knew we were both thinking the same thing. Claudia let out another soft cry, rolled over and went back to sleep. We both let out a sigh of relief and grinned at each other.

I leapt on her, unbuttoning my pants and pulling them down just enough to release myself. I wanted to be inside her so badly, I didn't bother to take them off. A groan of pleasure escaped my lips as I buried myself in her and she still felt like heaven.

"Look at me," I said in a half whisper, half grunt, and she turned her gorgeous face toward mine. I reached down and pulled her hair out of her face and tucked it behind her ear. She reached her hands up and grabbed the sides of my face, pulling me into a deep soulful kiss. Her body tensed beneath me, and I knew she was close. So was I.

"Let go," I whispered softly in her ear. She did as she was told and I followed her into bliss.

I laid beside her, and she snuggled herself into the crook of my arm and closed her eyes. I kicked off my pants and intertwined her legs with mine, buried my face in her fragrant curls and did the same.

"ALEX," Callie called to me groggily with suspiciously minty breath. "What is that god awful noise? Is that our wedding song?"

"It was." I sat up, rubbing the sleep from my eyes. "But I now think it's the song they'll play on repeat in Hell."

We went to the window and saw a boy with shaggy red

hair sitting on the path in front of the patio, playing a guitar, singing and looking into a window on the upper floor: Alexandra's window. Turning back to the kid, I recognized the smitten, besotted look on his face all too well. At least he had a gimmick, poor bastard.

I rubbed my eyes and walked down the hall to join my wife who was standing at Alexandra's door, which was her childhood bedroom.

I squeezed her shoulders gently as I stood behind her. Her arms were crossed and she glared at our second oldest daughter.

"Why is there a boy playing "Thinking Out Loud" on the guitar in the front yard?" she asked.

"That's Alistair." Alexandra called from the window where she was peering through the blinds. "We met at the wedding. He just graduated from Cambridge. He's here for a summer job at Scotiabank, then he's moving back to London to work for his father's brokerage firm."

It was a suspiciously large amount of information, which did nothing to answer my wife's question.

"I didn't ask who he was." My wife rolled her eyes. "I asked why he's *here*."

"Well," she smiled sheepishly, not taking her eyes off of the window. "Like I said, we met at the wedding, we talked for a while." She twirled a lock of dark curly hair around her finger as she paused, looking wistfully at the shaggy redhead, and I felt a knot forming in my stomach. "He asked me on a date and I said no."

I closed my eyes. It was happening.

"If you said no," Callie began in a slow patronizing tone. "Why is he here?"

"Well, he asked me again, and I said, if he brought his guitar and played a song on my front yard, I'd think about it."

"He's been out there for at least an hour."

"Well," Alexandra replied, "he came. He played a song. I thought about it, and I said no."

Callie and I rolled our eyes in unison.

"C'mon Lexi," I sighed. "Why would you do that if you knew you were going to say no?"

"I didn't think he would do it." She turned to look at us. "I don't want to go out with a guy who's just gonna leave at the end of summer. The same thing happened to my friend Jessica last year. She cried for weeks."

"But *you're* leaving at the end of the summer," I pointed out, "You're going back to Harvard."

"That's different." Alexandra rolled her eyes as if she'd explained everything.

Callie and I looked at each other and shrugged.

"Well, that doesn't explain why he's still here," Callie said. "Or why he's playing our wedding song."

"Well," she began again, turning back to the window. "I told him it was my favorite song." She was smiling again.

"He said he would keep playing it until I said I'd go to the movies with him."

The knot in my stomach had turned into a ball. The day I'd been dreading for nineteen years had come, and I had two more to look forward to.

"Well, this is inappropriate," her mom said, and gave me a wink. "If you don't want to go out with this boy, I think your father should go outside and get rid of him."

"I'm on it," I said, not even bothering to make a move for the door.

"No!" Alexandra turned.

My wife smiled.

"I mean, he's gonna leave soon anyway. What kind of idiot would stand outside someone's house singing all day just to get them to go out on a date?" She turned back to the window smiling.

Callie and I gave each other a knowing look. We walked toward the kitchen.

"I'll put on a pot of coffee," she said.

"Yeah." I kissed her and followed her down the stairs, "I'll go make the idiot a sandwich."

THE SOUNDTRACK

CHERISHING THE GODDESS

The Cherishing the Goddess playlist can be found here on Spotify

1. ISLAND IN THE SUN - HARRY BELAFONTE
2. GOING DOWN/ LOVE IN AN ELEVATOR - AEROSMITH
3. RUN THE WORLD (GIRLS) - BEYONCÉ
4. BEAUTIFUL BARBADOS - THE MERRYMEN
5. ROMANTIC CALL (FEAT. YO-YO) - PATRA, YO-YO
6. DRUNK IN LOVE - BEYONCÉ, JAY Z
7. YELLOW BIRD - THE MERRYMEN
8. I SEE FIRE - ED SHEEHAN
9. LOVE ON THE BRAIN - RIHANNA
10. CARO MIO BEN - GIUSEPPE GIORDANI
11. WUK UP ON IT - KING SHEPHERD
12. DIAMONDS - RIHANNA
13. SADDEST DAY - WAYNE WONDER
14. ISLAND WOMAN - THE MERRYMEN
15. LOVE ON TOP - BEYONCÉ

16. WE FOUND LOVE - RIHANNA, CALVIN HARRIS
17. THINKING OUT LOUD - ED SHEEHAN
18. GODDESS - ROSS DAVID

AUTHOR'S NOTE

Cherishing the Goddess was inspired by the song; "Thinking Out Loud" by Ed Sheeran.

CTG was originally a ten chapter novella published in May of 2018. This one of my favorite stories, even seeping into other books, and it never felt complete to me. At the time, I didn't think I could write longer stories but after writing and publishing Everything's Better With Kimberly, I decided to take another look at this one. When I did, the words came pouring out.

The settings are based loosely on real places in Barbados. The tourist locations are real and lovely and you should all visit, particularly Oistin's where the food is amazing.

Thank you:

My amazing critique partners: Marina Garcia & Miri Stone. Your encouragement and very honest opinions kept me going week to week while writing this beast.

My amazing beta readers who wouldn't let me quit halfway through, giving me inspiration, encouragement and making me fall in love with Adam & Kimberly as much as they did.

Tasha Harrison for editing, molding and shaping this story, twice. Thank you for answering my way too many emails and your brilliant insight and unending patience.

Romance Rehab, especially Jennifer, for your brilliant author services, particularly, the blurb critiques. I also hope I sell a bazillion copies!

Give Me Books Promotions, Inkslinger PR & Honey Magnolia PR for helping me spread the word guiding me seamlessly through the book marketing process.

Steamy Designs for the beautiful cover design. Thank you for taking my ideas and making them come to life.

My genius and brutally honest mother. Thank you for being my Alzheimer's technical advisor.

My ARC team for giving their time and energy to read my work and help spread the word.

Thank you so much, dear reader, for reading Cherishing the Goddess!

I hope you liked it. Please consider leaving a review wherever you share your good news!

xoxo,

lucy

April 2019

NOTES FROM PARADISE

THE LUCY EDEN NEWSLETTER

*S*ign up for my monthly newsletter

notes from paradise

Click the title to join the fun:

- info about my latest release
- an excerpt from my WIP
- a writing prompt contest
- giveaways
- my TBR & unsolicited book reccomendations
- and my favorite part, an exclusive short story or novelette

CLICK HERE TO SIGN UP OR VISIT LUCYEDEN.COM

ALSO BY LUCY EDEN

LUCY EDEN

EVERYTHING'S

better

WITH KIMBERLY

ONE

KIMBERLY

Okay, Kimberly, breathe. You got this. It's only an airplane. Airplanes fly hundreds of times a day, all day long. It's the safest way to travel.

I tried to keep calm and focus on the pep talk my brother, Cole, gave me when he dropped me off at the airport.

"You got this, Stringbean. You've flown dozens of times. Only this time, you'll be alone, which means you won't have to fight me for the armrest or sit in RJ's lethal gas clouds." RJ was our younger brother. The memory made me smile, but it did little to calm my mounting terror.

"Ma'am?" a female voice called to me and I jumped a mile when the flight attendant tapped me on the shoulder. "Are you all right?"

No, I am not all right. I'm terrified. I can't breathe, my heart is going to explode, and I'm pretty sure we are all going to die in this metal box being hurled into the air by science that I don't understand.

"Yes, I'm fine." I gave her a tight smile that felt more like a grimace. "Thank you for asking." She didn't seem convinced. "It's just that I don't fly very often and I'm a little nervous," I stammered, and I could feel tears stinging my eyes.

Damn it. She's going to think I'm a lunatic and throw me off the plane.

She gave me a pitying smile that I tried to return, but it felt like another grimace.

"I think I might be able to help you. Follow me." She moved toward the front of the cabin and I was sure she was going to lead me off the plane. I started to mentally calculate the best way to get to Barbados without flying.

I could drive to the tip of Florida and what? Would I charter a boat or swim?

Those ideas were crazy. Then I started thinking about how I would explain to my boss that I got kicked off of a plane on my way to work on my first international project. I struggled to keep my breath even when the flight attendant stopped and turned to face me.

"Here you are!" she called brightly. "We had an extra first class seat. It's a little more comfortable and spacious. It also comes with unlimited champagne. I'll bring you a glass."

"Thank you," I managed to eke out in a grateful whisper and sat down. After taking a deep breath, then another, I felt my heart rate slowly return to a normal pace.

"Nervous flyer?" a deep voice asked from the seat next to me.

"Yeah," I mumbled while fumbling with my seat belt. Once the seat belt was secure, I looked up and my breath caught in my throat.

Sitting in the other seat in my row was an impossibly gorgeous man.

He was broad shouldered and muscular with blonde hair and hazel eyes. Even though he was seated, I could tell he was tall. The warm smile he gave me revealed two rows of perfect teeth. It was momentarily hypnotizing. He chuckled at my expression. This man was probably used to having women react that way to his perfectly formed face with just the right amount of facial hair. I imagined myself running my fingers through the scruff on his cheek and chin before pressing my lips to —

"Your champagne, ma'am," the flight attendant inter-rupted my thoughts, curtly, and I wondered if she was annoyed because she was waiting for me to collect my drink or because I was staring at my seat mate. It was probably both.

"Thank you." I gave her my sweetest smile, took the glass from her hands and placed it on my tray table. Rolling my eyes, I dropped the smile as soon as her back was turned and sank back into my seat, continuing to try to regulate my breath.

"Aren't you going drink that?" the handsome man next to me inquired.

"It doesn't always help," I said quietly. "Sometimes, it makes it worse." I couldn't believe I'd just said that out loud. I didn't owe him an explanation but he seemed so genuinely concerned.

"How long have you been having panic attacks?" he asked matching my quiet tone.

Shocked, I turned to look at him. *How did he know?*

"I'm sorry. It's just that I used to see them all the time at school. I studied architecture at Pratt and it was pretty intense. One of my friends used to—"

Wait. Did he say he studied architecture at Pratt? He's also drop-dead gorgeous and on the same flight to Barbados? What were the odds?

"I'm sorry to interrupt you, but are you Adam Price?"

It was his turn to be shocked and he smiled again. "I am. How did you know that?"

The Man-Whore. I was sitting next to the Man-Whore.

"Just a guess." I shrugged.

"Well, I assume from your sudden change of expression my reputation precedes me."

My poker face needed some serious work. I tried to plaster on a professional smile. "You studied architecture at The Pratt Institute for both undergrad and grad school. You've worked on an impressive number of international projects before becoming the youngest senior architect at Will and Peking Design. Now, you're on your way to

Barbados to pitch WP for a hospitality project for Wolfe Industries."

"That's pretty impressive and spot on." He nodded appreciatively. "Who are you?"

"Thanks," I said with a nod, feeling like I'd dodged a very uncomfortable bullet. "I'm Kimberly Simmons. I work for Wolfe. I'll be working with you on the pitch."

I extended my hand to shake and he accepted, engulfing my dark slender hand in his huge pale one. It briefly reminded me of a Gap ad. My heart started to race again, but in a good way. This conversation had succeeded in drawing my attention elsewhere and I started to feel like myself again. I tried to withdraw my hand from his grasp and noticed he hadn't relinquished his grip, not that I minded. I'd make sure not to let him know that.

"And that's *all* you've heard about me?" His voice became a low, sexy growl.

My eyes narrowed and I steeled myself. I was prepared for this, though I didn't think I was his type. Maybe Man-Whores didn't have a type.

"No." I smiled innocently, pulling my hand back and placing it in my lap. "Is there anything else I should know?"

"Hmm." He smirked, but seemed thoroughly unconvinced.

We sat in awkward silence through the inflight announcements. I organized my laptop, headphones and tablet; all the things I brought to help me get through the flight. My hand briefly closed around the little plastic prescription bottle—that I hoped I wouldn't need—in the inner pocket of my tote, just in case. I glanced over at Adam and he was sketching on a large tablet with a stylus. It was a large rustic house with wood and stone exteriors. He'd created an odd combination of a log cabin, a ski chalet and a mansion, but it worked together beautifully. He caught me looking and smiled.

"You know," he said, smirking, "most people would consider it rude to read over someone's shoulder."

"You know," I replied, returning his sly smile, "most people would assume that someone who'd invest in an obnoxiously large tablet doesn't prioritize discretion."

"Discretion happens to be one of my specialties." His smile never faltered. I didn't answer him and was glad he couldn't tell I was blushing. "An *obnoxiously large tablet* is a requirement for the job," he said, mimicking me. "It's a passion project of mine. I plan on building it myself in Upstate New York." He held the large tablet out for me to see. I shot him a wary glance before looking down. It was breathtaking. He scrolled through the plans, explaining all the details and he sounded like a kid describing his favorite new toy.

"—an open floor plan, of course. These large kitchen windows would face east, so when I'm having breakfast in the morning I can watch the sunrise. The windows in the dining area," he scrolled to the next rendering, "would face the west for sunsets—" I'd never heard someone so excited about natural sunlight. It was very endearing.

No, Kimberly. You will not find the Man-Whore endearing.

"It's very nice." I said, giving him a small smile. Then I tried to focus on something else, anything else, but his forearm on my armrest, the way his eyes lit up when he described the atrium he was planning for the center of his house or the small playground in the backyard. I put in my earbuds and Sade began singing to me about a quiet storm. Closing my eyes, I drew in deep calming breaths. Then the plane started to taxi down the runway.

I forced my breaths to become longer and slower as I tried to recreate the breathing exercises Dr. Marquez recommended, but it did nothing to slow my heart rate. My heart was throwing itself against my chest as if it were trying to break through my ribcage. My body pressed into the seat back as the plane ascended, but instead of just feeling an incline, I felt like I was tumbling head over heels like Alice down the rabbit hole. I wanted to scream, and I must have made some sound of distress because my hand was suddenly encased in warmth.

"Hey!" It was Adam's voice.

I didn't feel him remove my earbuds. Sade wasn't singing anymore, and it sounded like he was calling to me from the end of a tunnel. The more he said my name, the louder and clearer his voice became.

"Hey, Kimberly. Look at me. Look. At. Me."

I forced my eyes open and turned to face him. His handsome face was calm but his eyes were full of concern.

"You're going to be fine."

That was easy for him to say. He wasn't dying.

"Just breathe."

I was *trying* to breathe.

"In through your nose."

I focused on his words and drew in a deep breath through my nostrils and held it.

"Out through your mouth." I did as he said.

"Again," he ordered, and breathed with me.

After five breaths, I started to feel a little better, but I was still spinning. Out of the corner of my eye, I saw the flight attendant approaching, her face full of apprehension. My heart started pounding again. Adam held up his hand and she backed away.

"Look at me. Stay with me."

He clasped my hand with both of his. I hoped he would never let go. I felt like his hands were the only things keeping me tethered to reality. If he let go, I would float away.

"What do you see?" he asked.

"What?" I managed to say but it sounded like a croak.

"Tell me what you see. Name five things that you see right now."

"I don't underst—"

"Just do it."

"I see, um, I see...a headrest." I forced myself to look at him again. He smiled and nodded to encourage me.

"That's one."

"Your tablet."

"That's two."

"Your eyes." *Damn it. Did I actually say that?*

"That's three." Then he grinned. "Are you flirting with me in the middle of a panic attack?"

"No, I'm not, I..." I stammered.

"Hey, I'm into it."

His golden brown eyes glittered with mirth. I laughed with him, more out of relief than anything else. I was starting to feel okay again. Every breath felt like a gift. My world was no longer spinning. I took a few sips of water and sat in silence for a long time, embracing the calm.

Adam held my right hand with his left, pulled out his tablet and read a book, like it was the most natural thing in the world. He didn't fuss over me. He didn't ask me if I was okay a million times. He didn't embarrass me. He just knew that I was all right and let me be, but still held my hand. It was the kindest thing anyone—who wasn't a relative— had ever done for me, and I was feeling guilty for judging him so harshly.

He will charm the panties right off of you. Be careful.

Was I being charmed? Was Adam Price taking advantage of a vulnerable woman? I was so grateful for him in that moment and I didn't want to believe that a person who could be so sweet and attentive to a total stranger could be so manipulative. I also didn't believe he would behave the same way if I were a man who'd just had a panic attack.

Adam Price wouldn't be the first to try to get into my pants; if that's what he was trying to do. I had to think about my career and I'd received very clear warnings about him. If I ignored them and ruined this opportunity, I'd only have myself to blame.

But it wouldn't hurt to hold his hand for a little while longer.

———

A LITTLE LONGER turned out to be the entire flight, with breaks for eating, a trip to the bathroom—one for him, one for me—and a couple of crossword puzzles. I also managed to nap for a couple of hours. He was holding my hand when I fell asleep and was still holding it when I woke up.

I felt a little guilty allowing myself to enjoy this hand holding for so long—a little less guilty when I got some major side eye from the flight attendant—but he had such a calming effect on me. Still, I didn't want to give him the wrong idea.

The landing was far less traumatic than the take off, and I couldn't be sure, but I think Adam was purposely trying to keep my focus on him.

"Please don't tell me you're one of those people who clap when the plane lands," he said with the corners of his mouth curling. He caressed the back of my hand with his thumb. It was sending waves of heat throughout my body. My cheeks flushed, my chest tightened and I felt a tingling between my thighs.

"What's the problem with giving the pilot a little appreciation for not killing us?" I tried to push every unprofessional thought about Adam Price out of my head.

The plane bumped to a relatively smooth landing. My hand tightened around Adam's as the plane taxied down the runway and came to a stop at the terminal. A burst of applause and cheers erupted from the rear of the plane. We turned to each other and cracked up. Our laughter died down and our gazes lingered for a moment too long.

Damn it.

"Thank you for coaching me through that panic attack," I said, then disembarked as quickly and politely as possible. I don't think I've ever moved so fast in my life. My carry-on suitcase bumped and bounced behind me as I made my way down the air-stairs and hustled across the tarmac, trying to put as much distance as I could between myself and Adam Price until I had to see him again at the meeting.

There were only three people ahead of me in the customs line and I couldn't be more grateful. The customs officer was incredibly efficient and within minutes I was making a beeline for the taxi stand.

I approached the curb and looked around for a taxi, realizing I wasn't quite sure how car services worked in Barbados.

"Do you need a ride?" Adam's voice called from behind me, and I swear I could hear him smiling.

How the hell did he get through customs so fast?

"No, thank you." I replied without turning around. "I can manage."

"If I didn't know any better," He put his hand on my shoulder. His touch made me shiver in eighty-degree weather, "I would think you were trying to avoid me." I turned to face him. He was smirking at me again, an expression I was beginning to find incredibly sexy.

No, Kimberly. You must not find the Man-Whore sexy.

"I'm not trying to avoid you." I dropped my bags and put my hands on my hips. "I just think it would be in our best interests if we kept things professional from now on."

His smile widened, threatening to give me another glimpse of his perfect white teeth. "Do you mind if I wait to make sure you get into a car?" He put his hands up in a defenseless posture. "...strictly as a professional courtesy."

"Thank you, but that's not necessary, Mr. Price."

Adam clutched his heart and staggered backwards causing my resolve to crack and eliciting a chuckle. His spot-on fake heart attack made me wonder if he'd also grown up watching *Sanford and Son* reruns.

"Mr. Price? Seriously?" he cried in feigned indignation. "Ugh. I thought I meant more to you than that."

"Could you stop that?" I hissed through clenched teeth

while fighting the beginning of a smile. A few heads turned in our direction. "You're making a scene."

"Let me give you a ride to your hotel," Adam offered again, dropping his voice to a normal volume.

I shook my head and dug my fists into my hips. "I already told you, I'll be fine."

"After all we've been through! How could —" He threw his head back and flung his arms wide, clearly winding up for another histrionic display.

"Okay, okay." I grabbed his arms and pulled them down. His biceps were firm against my palms. "You can drop me off at my hotel. Will you stop now?"

"If you insist, but please try to keep your hands to yourself. We are professionals after all." His eyes flicked downward to where my hands still gripped his biceps then back to mine. I pulled my hands away quickly, feeling my cheeks flush again.

Adam grabbed my rolling carry-on and walked toward a black SUV with tinted windows. He opened the door and held out his hand for me to use to climb inside. After a moment, he climbed in beside me. I half expected him to reach for my hand. I couldn't tell if I was more relieved or disappointed when he didn't.

"Where are we headed?" he asked.

I opened and closed my mouth a few times. Apparently, his proximity caused me to temporarily lose my ability to speak.

"Where's your hotel, Kimberly? We have to tell the driver…"

"Right, um." I shook my head in an attempt to regain my senses, grabbed my tablet, and opened my itinerary. "The Sterling Beachfront Paradise."

"Wait. Did you say The Sterling Beachfront Paradise?" Adam asked

I nodded.

"I'm also staying at The Sterling Beachfront Paradise."

"Bullshit." I glared at him.

He opened his tablet and handed it to me. I took it from him and discovered that he was telling the truth. A quick comparison of our reservations assured me that at least we weren't staying in the same building. I knew The Sterling was a big resort, with accommodations ranging from small hotel rooms to big luxury apartments. Most likely, we'd never run into each other.

I couldn't tell if I was more relieved or disappointed by this.

Damn it.

THANK you for reading this bonus chapter of Everything's Better with Kimberly. Visit <u>lucyeden.com</u>

EVERYTHING'S BETTER WITH YOU

A SHORT, SWEET & STEAMY NOVELLA

Abigail Moore is an aspiring jewelry designer by day and bartender at a popular upscale gentleman's club by night. She has her job, her jewelry, her best friend, Janie and not much else until she's swept off her feet by a sexy stranger with a secret.

Nathan Price is the heir apparent of NYC's powerful Price family empire. Determined to set himself apart from his powerful father, he becomes his own man but his father's influence cast a long shadow that he may not be able to escape until a sassy beautiful stranger shows him the light.

. . .

THIS STAND-ALONE NOVELLA HAS AN ALPHA, virgin, love at first sight, safe, no cheating with a guaranteed happily ever after & lots of steam.

MELTED

A SHORT, SWEET & STEAMY NOVELETTE

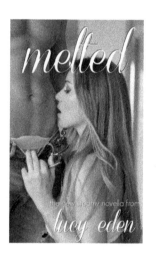

In a crowded social club in the heart of New York City full of the most successful and wealthy men in the country, Tessa Findlay grabs the attention of the wealthiest & also the sexiest.

So what does she do?

She panics and runs away, of course!

Charles Kerwin had everything in the world: money, success, fast cars, big homes and a giant bathtub. The one thing he didn't have: someone to share it with. That all changed the moment he laid eyes on the woman of his dreams, but she disappeared before he could talk to her.

So what does he do?

He buys the company she works for and moves to her hometown, of course!

THIS STAND-ALONE NOVELETTE is twenty-four hours of bat-shit crazy and has an obsessed alpha, love at first sight, no cheating with a guaranteed happily ever after.

PLEASE ENJOY with two pints of rum raisin on standby.

CAPTURING THE GODDESS

A SHORT, SWEET & STEAMY SHORT STORY

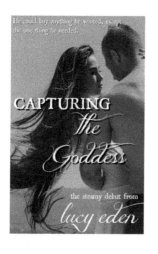

At twenty-eight, Trevor Edwards had thought he'd conquered the world. He had massive success in the art & corporate worlds, a happy marriage, and two gorgeous children. Then illness took his wife, and in her, he lost the mother of his children, his business partner, and his best friend. He's spent the next five years drifting through life, unknowingly searching for someone to fill the hole in his heart.

GAIA WESLEY WAS STRUGGLING art student. She's always held hope in her heart for a love that she wasn't sure exists, but a job interview with a reclusive widower can change everything.

THIS STAND-ALONE short story has an obsessed alpha, love at first sight, no cheating with a guaranteed happily ever after.

PLEASE ENJOY in a cozy corner of your favorite art museum.

CONQUERING THE GODDESS

A SHORT, SWEET & STEAMY SHORT STORY

Athena Anderson is young ambitious journalist fresh out of grad school & excited about her first assignment for Capital Exchange Magazine.

Grant Winters rules his corporate domain with an iron fist and has no time for distractions, like reporters from dried up media outlets.

Their first meeting doesn't go quite according to plan.

When they meet again sparks fly and maybe, a punch or two and Grant & Athena realize they have a lot more in common than they originally thought.

This standalone novella has an obsessed alpha, love at first

sight, safe, no cheating with a guaranteed happily ever
after.

ABOUT THE AUTHOR

Lucy Eden is the *nom de plume* of a romance obsessed author who writes the kind of romance she loves to read. She's a sucker for alphas with a soft gooey center, over the top romantic gestures, strong & smart MCs, humor, love at first sight (or pretty damn close), happily ever afters & of course, steamy love scenes.

When Lucy isn't writing, she's busy reading—or listening to—every book she can get her hands on— romance or otherwise.

She lives in New York with her husband, two children, a turtle & a Yorkshire Terrier.